Unveiling Love

A London Regency Suspense Tale: Episode III

Vanessa Riley

Books by Vanessa Riley

Madeline's Protector

Swept Away, A Regency Fairy Tale

The Bargain, A Port Elizabeth Tale, Episodes I-IV

Unveiling Love, Episodes I-IV

Unmasked Heart, A Regency Challenge of the Soul Series

Sign up at VanessaRiley.com for contests, early releases, and more.

Copyright © 2016 Vanessa Riley

Published by BM Books

A Division of Gallium Books

Suite 236B, Atlanta, GA 30308

ISBN-13: 978-1-943885-12-1

SAVING A MARRIAGE OR WINNING THE TRIAL OF THE CENTURY

Dear Lovely Reader,

Unveiling Love is a serialized historical romance or soap opera told in episodes. Each episode averages three to eight chapters, about 18,000 to 30,000 words. Each episode resolves one issue. Emotional cliffhangers may be offered, but the plot, the action of the episode, will be complete in resolving this issue.

My promise to you is that the action will be compelling, the romance passionate, and the journey like nothing you've read before. I will tell you in the forward the length. This episode, Episode III, is ten chapters long, 33,000 words. Enjoy this Regency Romance.

Vanessa Riley

Winning in the courts, vanquishing England's foes on the battlefield, Barrington Norton has used these winner-take-all rules to script his life, but is London's most distinguished mulatto barrister prepared to win the ultimate fight, restoring his wife's love?

Amora Norton is running out of time. The shadows in her mind, which threaten her sanity and alienate Barrington's love, have returned. How many others will die if she can't piece together her shattered memories? Can she trust that Barrington's new found care is about saving their marriage rather than winning the trial of the century?

In this episode:

Barrington Norton has always made the right decisions but desperation, lies, and unexpected truths make things go terribly wrong. Can London's top mulatto barrister protect Amora, himself, and their loved ones from ruin? How much will Barrington sacrifice to save the woman he loves?

Amora Norton has come to terms with her abduction and forgiven her Egyptian mother of betrayal, but hasn't the strength to do the same for Barrington or God. Can finding a lost friend and discovering an unexpected blessing be enough to make her whole?

Yet, all their efforts to solve the crime of the century may be for naught. A divided couple is the perfect prey for a criminal who needs all the sins wiped away.

Sign up for my newsletter at www.vanessariley.com or www.christianregency.com. Notices of releases, contests, my Regency Lover's pack, and other goodies will be made available to you.

Dedication

I dedicate this book to my copy editor supreme, my mother, Louise, my loving hubby, Frank, and my daughter, Ellen. Their patience and support have meant the world to me.

I also dedicate this labor of love to critique partners extraordinaire: June, Mildred, Lori, Connie, and Gail.

Love to my mentor, Laurie Alice, for answering all my endless questions.

Love to Sharon & Kathy, they made me feel the emotion. You're never second place in my heart.

And I am grateful for my team of encouragers: Sandra, Michela, Felicia, Piper, and Rhonda.

CAST OF PRIMARY CHARACTERS

Barrington Norton: a barrister by trade, he is a free-borne mulatto gentleman of a wealthy black merchant's daughter and a landowner's ne'er-do-well son.

Amora Norton: the wife of Barrington Norton. She is of mixed blood, the daughter of an Egyptian woman and a wealthy Spanish apple merchant.

Henutsen Tomàs: Amora's Egyptian mother.

Smith: a man convicted of coining.

Cynthia Miller: a songstress and sister of Gerald Miller.

Gerald Miller: Barrington's best friend who saved his life during the Peninsula War.

Mr. Beakes: Barrington's solicitor.

Vicar Wilson: a minister serving at St. George.

Duke and Duchess of Cheshire: the newly married interracial couple William St. Landon and Gaia Telfair, reformers.

Mrs. Gretling: an abigail to Amora.

James: a man-of-all-work to Barrington.

Mr. Charleton: a rival of Barrington from their youth.

Mr. Hessing: Barrington's mentor and barrister colleague.

Hudson Solemn: Barrington's cousin.

Chapter One: Amora to The Rescue

The cup of warm tea mother made from the peppermint leaves sat on Amora's bed table. If she sipped it, the potion would make her eyes heavy and her lids droop, but sleep was not what she wanted. Every nerve was on edge. Barrington hadn't come home.

A groan welled inside. Why was she worrying about him? The man was levelheaded, detail oriented, and decisive. That's why he couldn't understand weakness or desperation.

She blew out a breath, hoping the air would leach her system of longing - of wanting his laugh in her ear, his kiss on her lips.

A shiver swept over her, tightening about her middle as she remembered how sweet he'd been taking her on the balcony to distract her from Papa's loss. So kind and protective. So Barrington.

Did his pride hurt when she refused a last kiss?

Oh, how she wanted to weaken.

If not for that irksome Cynthia, she might've surrendered to the heat in his eyes, that fleeting promise of not being alone. He'd be with her now holding her, loving her to distraction, not lost to the outside world.

She glanced back at her perfectly creased sheets, allowing her heart to remember the last time she let him in her bedchamber. The memory -- his breathing in rhythm with hers, his hands, rough and strong drawing her closer and closer -- raced her heart. Right now, the jingle of his buttons on a divested waistcoat would be music to her lonely soul.

Yet when morning came, would anything change? He still wouldn't understand her fears. She'd always be otherworldly to him and to herself.

She counted her fingers and paced again. Images of Barrington robbed or hurt in a carriage accident filled her brainbox. She rubbed her temples and tried to focus on the gnarled bedpost, but the smooth empty sheets of her bed taunted her as well.

Nothing but Barrington could calm her soul. Her thoughts whirled and whirled. She kidded herself thinking she'd be well without Barrington. Feeling weak-minded and angry at him for staying out late and making her fret, she lunged forward to pound the wall but missed.

Swaying, she caught the window sill. She blinked her dizzy eyes, but the world continued to spin. Breathing in and out, she waited for the bad thoughts twisting inside to slip away.

Resigning her waiting, she pressed an ear to the window glass and listened for hope.

Silence.

A deathly stillness.

Not even a lone horse's clip-clop.

Where was Barrington?

Had he found Sarah?

What if the monster killed him like he promised to?

Again, she paced. Her teeth chattered thinking of the monster hurting Barrington. Her muscles coiled tighter. "Oh, Barr, come home."

Knock. Knock.

The sound upon her door made her flinch with happiness. He was here, outside her room. He was alright. She cinched up her thick woolen robe and ran to the entry.

Flinging open the door, she felt her heart shrivel and fall back to the bottom of her chest.

Her mother stood there, dressed for bed with curl papers in her hair. "Amora, I wanted to make sure you were alright. Is the tea helping?"

"I'm well. You needn't be concerned."

Mama pushed her way inside. "I am concerned."

Amora folded her arms tighter about her chest. She needed to prepare for the tongue lashing that only Henutsen Tomàs could bring. "Truly. Be at ease, Mother. I'm just tired."

The woman looked around then rubbed her chin. Her onyx black hair with hints of salt glistened about the stark white papers.

Was it Amora's imagination or was she putting more effort into her appearance for tomorrow's outing with the vicar than the Hessing's ball?

Mama came closer. "What if we stay a little longer? Being here in London hasn't been so bad. Even Barrington hasn't been so bad."

Feeling her forehead crinkle with suspicion, Amora patted her brow, then leveled her shoulders. "We have seven days left. You might change your mind."

Mama sighed. A look of defeat swept over her. She frowned her lips. "I've been wrong about many things, even Barrington. He loves you, you know? Why not give him another chance? With more time you may find more reasons to love than wrongs to hate."

Amora bristled on the inside. She moved to her bedframe and rubbed the smooth sheet as if it had wrinkles. "Things have been good between us, Mama. Let's not argue."

Mama came to her side and caught her fingers. "Is it good because I tell you what you want to hear? Is it good because I keep my opinions to myself?"

Amora straightened and glanced directly into her mother's coal-colored eyes. "Frankly, yes."

She released Amora's hand as if she'd touched burning kindling wood. "I know you haven't forgiven me, but at least you talk to me. Maybe you will listen and not close your ears this time."

"I've forgiven—"

"Vicar Wilson has told me of forgiveness. It's not this. Careful words, feeling trapped or scared. Always reminded of my sins. No, that can't be forgiveness."

Amora fanned heat from her face and glared at the petite fireball. "Careful, Mama. You're cavorting with the vicar's and Barrington's God. Your Isis one may hear and strike."

"Why?" The woman's brow rose as her tone lowered. "Why do I need to worry about a piece of wood's wrath when I have yours?"

"What?"

"Amora, saying you forgive is different than being forgiven. Who would Papa say was *a la mula*?"

Amora covered her mouth and backed away from the

truth. Barrington knew the difference between being loved and just craving safety. Surely, her mother could tell the difference in pretending to forgive to claim an ally. "Forgiv—"

Amora blinked her eyes hard as nausea flooded her stomach. The weakness must originate from her stubborn heart and neither would quit. She scooted to her vanity, dropped to her knees and lowered her face into the wastebasket. Mrs. Hessing's foul fowl dinner and maybe breakfast flowed out.

Amora wasn't sure how much time passed. Footsteps came and went as she knelt. Maybe she needed this cleansing to rid the anger caught up in her bones. It wasn't right to hold Mama and Barrington in bondage. It just wasn't.

When the heaving stopped, she sat back and dropped against Mama's legs. The woman's strong fingers had scooped up her loose hair to keep the locks from soiling. "My sweet *Ala mula*, you'll feel better in a moment."

She patted a cold damp cloth across Amora's neck. It felt wonderful.

Mama lowered a cup that smelled of roses. "Rinse your mouth with this."

Amora washed bitterness from her tongue. It was time to let some of the awfulness be rinsed away. She took in a long cooling breath and released the words she never wanted to say again. "I'm sorry."

Her mother smiled for a moment then brushed at her eyes. The coal pupils shimmered as if relieving the weight of condemnation had turned them to diamonds.

Mama helped her stand and plopped her atop the mattress. She wiped at the stream of water drizzling down Amora's damp cheek. "I need you too. Please, let us be friends."

She nodded and put her arms about Mama's hips, smashing her tired head against her stomach. "I want to try forgiveness. You may have to remind me everyday."

"Write one of your notes. The ones you read each morning."

Amora nodded and strengthened her hold.

Mama lifted her chin. "Amora, you do know why you've been so sickly as of late?"

Her mother's gaze pierced deep into Amora's imprisoned mind, the place she locked away truth and forgiveness.

"Mama, you think I am increasing, too?"

Her mother nodded her chin, as the prison guards in Amora's head, denial and self-pity took leave.

She put a palm to her flat, needed-to-be-empty stomach. "I can't be. That would mean three months, almost four."

"We'll know soon. I want you to talk with Barrington. Invite him in this room and don't come out until you both have an understanding. I've sent Mrs. Gretling home, and I'm going to have a long deep sleep with my special tea. You two will be able to scream at each other or love on each other. Fix this before you can't."

Surely it was too late for her and Barrington. He wasn't here anyway. She shook her head. "He and I aren't good at talking."

"Even better. Sometimes words get in the way. I saw the vulture that's after him. Don't let the loose Miller woman pick at his bones. Don't allow him think you no longer care."

She drew Amora forward and kissed her brow. "Don't be *a la mula*. Be love."

Mama headed to the door. She glanced back. "I won't side against you ever again, but I won't be silent anymore. Get your husband back."

The door closed, but mother's rebuke stayed.

Amora rubbed her arms and stared at the moldings framing the door. How could she be love when it always disappointed or was cruelly taken away?

Another sleepless hour passed. Amora closed her eyes at least a hundred times, but couldn't submit to tiredness. Her mother's hints kept repeating in her ear, the part about getting your husband back, the vulture part, not the ones of increasing-with-child.

Her stomach hadn't gotten bigger. The nausea, the weakness, all had to be from a prolonged winter cold and a poor dinner.

She stroked the empty pillow beside her and drew it to her chest. His pillow. Where was Barrington?

She kept hoping to hear him settling into his chambers, but heard nothing. No sound. No shuffle. Nothing.

He still hadn't made it home. Where was he?

Didn't he know she would be in a state waiting for him?

No, maybe he didn't.

She tossed the pillow and drew up from the mattress, bringing her knees to her. Everything sounded of silence. Coldness. Emptiness.

What if Cynthia took up Amora's challenge to seduce Barrington? What if she waylaid him into an errand and finally sunk her claws into his neckcloth?

Amora froze and slapped her palms together. *Oh, let him not be with that viper.*

She drew her palms to her temples and blocked her eyes. Her husband was honorable. Something had to be wrong.

She leaned over and pulled her candle closer. The orange flame with hints of blue danced upon the wax. Calm needed to fill her, so when Barrington showed unharmed, hopefully with their vows intact, he wouldn't find her worn as a fraying thread from fret. Or worse, having lost control of her reason.

Tip tap. She clapped her nails against the bronzed holder and sniffed the scent of char and dribbled wax.

A creak sounded.

Another noise, maybe a door closing whispered from below.

She heard heavy footfalls. Someone had entered the house, but not through the front unless she'd missed carriage noises. Barrington?

Juggling her heavy Dresden rhinoceros statue and candlestick, she rushed to her threshold, turned the knob and slipped to the stairs.

The lower level remained dark. Breathless and scared, she let her heart push her forward.

Her bare feet slapped against the treads, beating back each hesitation, each excuse she'd have to offer of why she was up and fretting. She had to see if he was well.

A sigh burst from her lungs when she spied light edging Barrington's study. He must be home. How did she miss his carriage? Did someone drop him home, through the rear, perhaps? Discreet Cynthia?

With another sigh, she pivoted to return to her chambers, then swiveled back. She had to see his face. Whatever he'd done, or wherever he'd been didn't matter as much as knowing all was well with Barrington. And, that he wasn't injured.

She trudged down the hall, humming away her angst. *Amazing Grace. How sweet...* She timed her steps, her breathing, her ramping jealousy to the rhythm. Once at the threshold, she filled her lungs and pressed on his door opening it.

Her gaze locked onto Barrington. He paced within. He kept moving as if he hadn't noticed her.

Her happy heart beat louder and louder, for the man didn't seem injured. But...

Ruined tailcoat.

Heavy breathing.

Something was wrong.

Her insides stilled. She gasped, clearing fear from her throat.

His gaze lifted. Wide, bloodshot silver eyes met hers.

The situation had to be dire. "What's afoot?"

He stopped, yanked at his cravat and plodded toward her. Without a word, he took the Dresden and candle from her fingers and stuck them on a nearby shelf. He snatched her off her feet and held her close, smashing her against his chest.

Wanting nothing other than saving him, she wrapped her arms around him.

His heart thudded wildly against her bosom. He smelled of dirt and sweat. What had he been doing? "Pray, tell me what is wrong."

"I..." His muscles quaked within her grasp. "I've ruined us."

She held him tighter, fingered the tension in his shoulders. "That can't be. Not Barrington Norton."

He pulled away as if she'd cut him. Clutching the bookcase, he opened his mouth wide, then grimaced.

"I'm not perfect. I never claimed to be."

Always in control, he'd never looked bewildered or scattered before.

She came to him, drawn by pure need. This time, it was him who lacked. Him who was in want of strength. "I didn't mean it as censure."

As she soaked up the tumult swimming in his eyes, she knew she had just enough strength to give. "Trust me, Barr. Trust in me."

He rubbed his brow and bowed his head, avoiding her question-filled gaze. "I took him. I stole him from Bedlam."

She stepped up on Mrs. Gretling's low chair, the one she used for dusting. Eye to eye, she held his face, clasped his shoulder. "You took whom?"

"Gerald Miller. He's alive." His face held no laughter. His darting eyes filled with a rawness matched by the gruffness of his voice. "I just took him from Bedlam."

"Alive? You took him?"

"Yes. I abducted him. I'd never jest about a word that has corrupted us."

Could it be so? Could Barrington be correct about Mr. Miller living?

He pressed her fingers deeper into the line of his jaw as if her touch could save him. "I know I'm not making sense. Bear with me. Just steady me."

Gladly. With her other palm, she cupped his chin. "Barr, I'm listening."

"I can't believe he's alive. But, it is Miller. My friend is alive."

"You said he died in the war."

His lips twisted, almost in a smirk. "I say a lot of things that turn out to be wrong. I tell you, he's alive.

And, I took him from Bedlam. I...I slid the chains from his hands. I stole him from Bedlam before Beakes and his dogs could seize him."

Bedlam? The place they put otherworldly people? She pulled his face near hers. She needed to hear him say the words again. "You stole a man from Bedlam?"

Barrington closed his eyes. "I need a room there or in Newgate for what I've done. If... no, when word gets out, we are all ruined."

If Gerald Miller were alive, then maybe Amora did hear his voice during her captivity. Maybe she wasn't as crazed as she thought. She blinked heavily and focused on the grim lines of Barrington's frown. "Where is he now?"

"Downstairs in the cellar, the servants' quarters. I had no other place to take him. Forgive me for putting all of us at risk. My father ruined my mother with his thoughtlessness. Now, I've made this house unsafe for you. I so wanted this place to mean safety for you."

The anguish in his voice melted the thawing ice she'd encased about her heart. With a tug at his dusty tailcoat, she wrapped her arms around his neck and held on until the vein along his throat stopped pulsing. "Barrington Norton, you've done nothing wrong. You aided a friend. There is so much good in that."

"The runners are after him for murder. Miss Druby's murder. Your Miss Druby. He's involved in this dark mystery. Is he the one, Amora?" He slipped his palms up her shoulders. His bloodshot eyes looked as if they'd pop. "Is he your monster?"

Pounding.

The knocks sounded from the outer door.

"Is he, Amora?"

She didn't want to think about that evil, not with Barr in trouble. "Someone's here. At this hour?"

The heavy hits started again.

Barrington startled as if he'd just heard the knocking and stepped away from her. "Perhaps someone followed us. I thought James was careful."

With a deep breath, he wiped at his forehead. "That may be the runners or Beakes coming to inform me that Miller's missing or to haul me away. How am I to get through this?"

"Don't answer. It's late."

He swung her from the chair, placed her feet gently to the floor. "I was supposed to meet Beakes. I…"

Shadows washed over his face, flattening his lips. His tell-tale cheek vibrated. "Just a minute."

His raised voice barely rose above the blood rushing her ears. Barrington was in trouble. He could be imprisoned like her.

She shook her head and gripped him by the lapels. "No. Don't."

"I have to answer. I don't know what else to do."

She tugged on his sleeves, stripping him of his coat. "Don't go dressed as if you just came in."

He nodded and let her slide off his cravat and drop it to the floor. Popping buttons, pulling at lacings, she opened his shirt and waistcoat. Her fingers skirted across the solid muscles of his back as she pulled the linen up over his head.

He could be sent to Newgate. And all she could do was stare at him, the beautiful leanness of the man, the thick arms that should always hold her through the night.

Collecting her wits, she yanked his heavy brocade robe

from a hook on the back of the door, then tossed it to him. "Put this on. You'll look as if you've just awakened."

He did so without any questions as if he accepted her commands as the best course of action.

Quickly, she whipped off his slippers then swept off his stockings. "Don't give anything away."

"As best as I can, but I don't lie. Pretty hard to start now."

Clad in just evening pantaloons and his robe, he grabbed her and left the study. "Please, stay here."

He closed the door, but all she wanted to do was go with him and face this trouble at his side. He looked too shaken to avoid incriminating himself. Avoiding detection, that was her gift. She'd have to help him, whether he wanted her to or not.

The door seemed miles away, or maybe Barrington just wished it was that far. Marching slowly as if he were part of the King's funeral guard, he moved toward the pounding.

Lord, don't let Mrs. Gretling or my mother-in-law awaken. They didn't need to see him hauled away. No, the pharaoh shouldn't have that image in her head.

The incessant knocking had to be Beakes and a very mad version of the bloodhound at that. "Just one more minute."

He schooled his face trying to remember how much was at stake. Amora seemed calm, as if she didn't care about how bad things could get. However, he knew what was at stake -- disgrace, imprisonment, confiscation of everything of value.

His judgments put her at risk. That frightened Barrington most of all. Right now, he didn't know himself.

Not wanting to be tossed in Newgate tonight, he swallowed a shaky breath and unbolted the door.

"'Bout time, Norton."

Beakes's ashy countenance seemed dark. Anger or a stiff pint flowed through him.

Barrington waved him inside. "Enter Beakes. But please, Mayfair is a quiet neighborhood."

The solicitor barreled into the townhouse. The man's heavy steps shook the floor. Barrington considered the possibility of the floor opening and dropping Beakes through. Having the man who could have him jailed fall into the cellar where Miller hid would be an even bigger disaster.

With a shake of his head, Barrington stepped around Beakes, lit a wall sconce and then headed for the parlor. "Follow me, but make less noise. You'll wake up everyone."

The man shrugged. "We didn't get him. The man calling himself Miller is gone."

His solicitor paced and shoved his big hands into his long coat. "He's gone. What a clever criminal."

Barrington moved to the mantle lighting candles and praying. Yes, lots of praying - for sanity, escape, and the return of his senses. "Are you sure it was him?"

"Yes, Norton. I hate bein' made a fool."

With nothing else to light, he set down Amora's candle and pivoted. He folded his arms, hoping to cover his shaking fingers. "Do you suspect someone informed him of danger?"

Beakes leaned against the sofa, sitting on the arm. "Obviously. I don't like anyone makin' me a laughing stock."

Barrington eased himself into a chair. A little twinge of pain from his hip reminded him that he wasn't used to lugging bodies. He kept the complaint to himself. How was he to get rid of Beakes from his townhouse? "Tell me how it was done."

"I don't know that much, Norton. All my sources said he was there."

Barrington dipped his chin, appearing to contemplate each word. Yet, the only thing his head wished for was escape or an earthquake. He cleared his throat of fret. "Perhaps, he's just misplaced. Bedlam is a large place."

"We searched the whole hospital. Nothing."

Barrington pounded a tight fist into his palm. He'd act like an innocent upset barrister. "This is terrible. What else has been done to find the man Miss. Miller believes to be Miller?"

"I put some of my runners on this. They will find him. The boy on watch said the last visitor he recognized was the singer."

The young lad didn't expose Barrington. Then why was Beakes here if he were not suspicious. Shaking his head as an innocent man would do, he decided to interrogate Beakes. "What led you to this suspect, this character at Bedlam? Is it possible you were deceived?"

The man guffawed and pulled out his gold pocket watch. "I lost a whole evening on this." A furrowed brow rose. "Just come from the magistrates explaining why I had him leave his bed for a hoax. I thought you were to meet us there." His solicitor popped up and came near. His shadow crowded Barrington's. "It was odd that you didn't show at the magistrates. What happened to you, Norton?"

Lies never left Barrington's lips, and they wouldn't

tonight. He stared straight into the man's eyes. "Something came up."

Beakes came even closer. "The singer is a friend of yours. You, your wife and Miss Miller, you're all from Clanville. You sure you didn't let something slip at Hessing's party? Something that showed our hand?"

Barrington leapt up, as if affronted. He stood ramrod straight. "Why would I do that? I don't want her involved in this situation."

"No, I don't suppose you want your ladybird involved with a murderer. That escapee from Bedlam is one, and he might be the biggest fiend of all, the Dark Walk Abductor. You wouldn't want to miss a chance at that prosecution. Your boss, Hessing, wouldn't. Not even for a good mistress."

Anger churned in Barrington causing a new shake to his hands. It wasn't just for the accusation of infidelity. Had he just helped the worthless dung who hurt Amora? If true, he'd kill Miller before the Crown could get the chance. "I want the Dark Walk Abductor to hang."

Barrington's voice echoed in the silent room.

Beakes backed up. Scratching his chin, the solicitor strutted in a circle. He stopped and faced Barrington. "The villain should pay as well as anyone helping him."

"Y-E-S!"

Barrington meant every letter of the word.

Yes, to stopping the villain.

Yes, to seeing the white hood draped on his head, and the platform floor drop away.

Yes, to giving all his victims peace.

Maybe seeing someone pay for hurting women would save Amora, too.

More than a half-year ago, the inmate, Smith had

been hung for his dealings with the fiend. The more he learned of the Dark Walk Abductor, the less guilty he felt over Smith's hanging. He gritted his teeth. "Anyone who helped the fiend hurt any woman should pay the ultimate price."

Eyes wide, Beakes stared at him. His cheeks lightened as if Barrington's words had sobered him. "That sounds personal. Good."

Shoving his fists into his pocket, he made his voice even and slow so the solicitor would catch his meaning and implied threat. "Righting wrongs is personal. Hessing taught me everything I know. I want justice. I want to be the man to finish the Dark Walk Abductor. No one will stop me."

Beakes looked down at the floorboards and kicked the rug's fringe with his boot. "What came up to deter you?"

"Sweetheart, are you coming back to me?" Amora's voice, full of seduction and mystery blew into the parlor like a wet kiss.

Both men pivoted toward the threshold.

She stood there. Her glorious hair flowed down, with a few curls obscuring an eye. A blanket draped her body but a naked shoulder and two bare ankles glistened in the candlelight.

Her violet eyes stretched as if they'd pop. "Oh my!"

She tried to cover up, yanking and pulling at the wool. Her attempts made it worse, exposing more skin.

He ran to her and bundled her beneath his robe. "Beakes, can we continue this in my office at the Lincoln Inn? I seem to have my hands full."

"I... You do have them full." The man's cheeks darkened. He covered his eyes and plodded to the door. "Good night, Mr. Norton. Mrs. Norton."

The door closed. Barrington let all the tired, frustrated, enraged, enraptured air out of his lungs. When the sounds of a fleeing carriage disappeared, he stepped back from the embrace heating his numb insides. Moving away from Amora to the entry, he bolted the door and returned to their shared threshold. Laying his head against the white trim, he stared at the woman standing before him.

Confident, blanket clinging to her bosom.

So beautiful and determined.

He pushed at his spectacles, mainly to ensure that his eyes weren't deceitful. "Thank you for chasing away Beakes. But did you have to expose yourself?"

"It worked, Barrington. You're safe."

The blanket slid again from her creamy neck. He stepped close and tugged it back into place. Another mistake, for his fingers stayed on her shoulder. As if glued to her soft skin, his hand couldn't be moved. "How was this show a good idea?"

A smile, tiny but beautiful, crossed her lips. "I've hidden my problems for five years. I didn't think you had enough practice to fool that determined hound."

Was his mouth curled up from her humor or the desire to find out if she truly came from his study in merely a blanket? His thumb hooked onto the wool. It wouldn't take much effort to discover the truth. "Well, you've given Beakes a story that will keep him for a while. Now return to your chambers. I'll puzzle this out."

Her smile faded as if he'd insulted her. "I want to help. I'm here to help."

He shook his head and woefully recalled his fingers. "I can't get you more entangled."

"Oh. It seemed like you needed me. It felt good to

help." Her hand balled as she pulled on her blanket. "I must've been mistaken. Barrington Norton doesn't need anyone, especially not his lunatic—"

He grabbed her and took her lips before she could whisper another horrid and untrue word. He didn't mean to startle Amora, but he needed her. The feel of her in his study calmed his rage, ordered the confusion in his head. Unnerved, he might have confessed to Beakes.

She was leaning into him now. Her arms locked about his neck. "Oh, Barr."

She'd purred his name, that throaty way she did when he got his passion right, right timing, right way to dip her backwards to deepen the kiss.

Yes, tasting his name upon her mouth, felt good. It was cleansing.

Three months of not kissing her, of not having her arms about his neck clinging to him. Their breathing in rhythm...

Her familiar lilac scent invaded his lungs, smashing the self-control in his brainbox. His fingers delighted in touching what was his, what should always be his.

She should never have doubts about his love and desire for her, none. He slid an arm along her curves, picked her up and headed into the parlor to the soft sofa. No doubts, no separation would remain.

"Barr. Please." She pushed at his chest. "Let's go to Miller."

That didn't quite sound like an invitation. And one kiss or four or five couldn't solve all their problems, not with a live "dead" friend in the cellar and her leaving at week's end.

He set her feet along the floor and took a step backward, placing cold, unheated distance between them. "You saved me. You did. But, I don't know what good it will do. I've stolen a man, a possible murderer and abductor and put him in our cellar."

"Take me to him, Barr. I need to see him. There are pieces of my memories that are just within my grasp. I know Gerald Miller is a part of them."

"Miller could be your abductor. Ask me to cut off an arm rather than bring you to danger."

She looked at the floor. "I have to see him." Her voice lowered to whispers. "It won't hurt me. It will help me remember. I have to remember."

If he denied her, Barrington knew she wouldn't see it as his duty to protect her. No, she'd take it as more evidence of his lack of faith in her. He gripped the sash of his robe and tightened it. "If you're going to keep helping, please dress. I'm having trouble keeping my mind on Miller. It keeps picturing you and that sofa and no blanket."

Her eyes went wide. She nodded. A grin popped onto her face as she traipsed down the hall.

He watched her hips sway as she went into his study. His insides churned anew. Allowing her to *help* would probably become another one of his regrets, on his ever growing list.

And she was definitely bare beneath the blanket.

Chapter Two: Seeing The Past

Amora never went to their cellar, any cellar. She clung to Barrington's arm as he led her down the steps.

He stopped halfway down. "What would your mother say if she knew I was getting you more involved?"

She thought about mentioning mother's other advice about not talking, but that wasn't a safe idea. Not with his kisses still smoldering on her lips and a huge chunk of the mystery hiding below. She nodded as she tugged him forward. "Mother's sleeping very heavily tonight, so she won't find out."

Further down the staircase, it became darker and much harder to breathe. She wasn't afraid to confront Mr. Miller. Her angst was the unknown, the pieces of her memories she couldn't grasp. "If this is truly Mr. Miller, then my memory of him calling out my name had to be real. That would mean he was there."

Barrington looked tense like he did before big trials. His eyes darted over his glasses. "Yes, it would. And a whole bunch of other questions."

She didn't care so much of other questions just one

more answer. Maybe she wasn't so otherworldly.

Maybe it was safe to believe in herself again.

"Amora, are you suffering?"

She blinked and looked up at Barrington.

His eyes were wide. He looked ready to pounce upon anything amiss. "I said your name twice. You didn't respond."

"I was a little sick this evening. Couldn't keep dinner down. Horrible dinner."

"You've been sickly lately. Would it be of use to have a doctor look at you? I've reached out to my cousin from my mother's side of the family. You remember Hudson Solemn. He's just settling back from living in India. His methods would be different."

"No doctors, especially your hateful cousin. He doesn't like me."

"He doesn't like or dislike you. He mistrusts everyone."

She slid her hand to his palm, lacing her fingers with his. "Never mind him. Seeing Miller will be all the good I need."

They took a few more steps, then he spun her to him. "A month of stomach troubles? Amora, do you trust me enough to tell me anything? Even strain? Don't suffer in silence. Don't pretend anymore."

Barrington's gaze was so warm. It held no pity. She felt valued and protected. Did he still love her after all they'd been through? After she'd rejected his every offer to make amends?

"I would, Barr. Like you would have told me about Mr. Miller."

He looked over his glasses again. "Well, he's here."

"He must know where I was held captive. He may even know the identity of my tormentor."

"Amora?" His spectacles askew. His robe hung disheveled. He'd never looked more handsome. "What if...? Wait—"

"We can't stop now." She started down the steps again and prepared her mind for seeing Gerald Miller. What would be her first reaction?

To shout?

To cry?

To crumble?

Her footing slipped a little as she took the next step. Now wasn't the time to lose her wits. Latching more tightly to the railing, she hummed the song Barrington taught her in Hyde Park.

Down the hall, past the wine cellar, he stopped at a closed door and moved in front of her. He gazed at her as if he saw her for the first time. Maybe seeing her with determination was different. "If this is too much, we can make this short. Or, I could take you now to your room. I'll carry you there. Maybe whisper sweet nothings."

"Barr, stop joking. I'm fine. Mrs. Hessing needs better cooks. We go together. Unity."

"I don't know how he's alive, Amora. Did he desert? How did he get from the battlefield to Bedlam? Is he a murderer like Beakes said? Did he hurt you?"

Murderer? Not kind Mr. Miller, Barrington's loyal friend. She reached up to touch her husband's jaw. "Breathe, the answers will come."

He kissed her palm. "Wise woman."

Rolling back his thick cuff, he knocked upon the door. "It's Norton."

A frowning James answered. "Ma'am?" Waving a sloshing mug of coffee, he blocked the entry. The brown liquid splashed, staining his livery about his lapel.

The stench of coffee filled the air, clogging her throat. She grabbed the molding framing the door, her voice a whisper. "James, we came to see Mr. Miller."

Barrington grabbed the mug. He slid it passed her nose.

She wrinkled her nose and kicked her head backwards. Now wasn't the time to vomit.

Half-smiling, Barrington put the cup to his lips. After a big gulp of the noxious potion, he wiped his mouth. "Sorry, James. I needed something to make me more alert."

"Sir, ma'am. I have things under control here. You should both retire."

Barrington put an arm about her waist. "I've already offered, but she won't go. She knows everything."

The strength in his big arm made her steady. She leaned into him, righting her dizzy mind. "We must see, Mr. Miller."

James seemed hesitant. His gaze flickered from her to Barrington.

"All is well for now, James. And Mrs. Norton just creatively saved my hide."

His voice lowered, kissing her ear. "We should discuss your methods in detail later." He pursed his lips and let his gaze wash over her. "There's a great deal we need to discuss."

In the candlelight, Barrington's eyes glittered. It didn't seem like a lecture would be forthcoming.

"Yes, sir. He's got the shakes real bad. Real bad." James nodded his chin as he moved aside. "I'll wait by the door."

Barrington slowly lifted his fingers from her middle and let Amora slip into the room.

A gasp bubbled from her mouth before she could stop it. The whitewashed bedchamber seemed smallish like the asylum she'd been sent to.

"Amora?" A frown fell upon his lips. "If this will cause too much strain, I won't let you stay."

"I'm well. I've never been down here."

She tiptoed to the mattress upon which Mr. Miller laid. Linen draped his thin frame. His emerald eyes lay open. She waved her hand over his face.

Nothing, no movement or hint of awareness. Could he see the boards forming the low ceiling?

Did he know she and Barrington were there and just couldn't respond? His body twitched. She stepped away.

"What's wrong with him?"

Barrington stepped beside her. "Miller, awaken! Tell us how you are alive?" He started to shake his best friend. "I saw the lead ball tear into your chest. How is this possible?"

She pulled at Barrington's wild hands. "Stop. He won't answer if you further scramble his brainbox."

"I just need answers, Amora. I don't like so many questions."

Gerald Miller's eyes moved. In a shaky voice, he mumbled something.

Barrington put his ear close. "Say it again, Miller."

This time the moan was louder. "M. Tomàs safe."

Barrington's face became ashen. "What about Miss Tomàs?" He gripped Miller's thin shoulder as if he'd rip them apart. "What about Amora Tomàs? What about her? Why are you asking?"

The anguish and confusion in her husband's voice was thick. It wrenched her heart. From behind, she wrapped her arms about him. "Let Miller go. He's unconscious again."

Barrington struggled for another moment then backed away from the bed. He pivoted and scooped her into his embrace. "Why is he talking about you?"

She lifted her chin and caught his hurting stare. "Because he was there. I remember hearing his voice where the monster kept me. But, you said he died on the battlefield."

He set her on a stool, then started to pace. His bare feet slapped the ground with each pivot. "You'd mentioned being confused over voices and people. Oh, why didn't I listen? I wouldn't have set Beakes onto Miller thinking he was a fraud."

Barrington stopped. His shoulders slouched as he leaned over the bed again. "Beakes thinks he killed Miss Druby, the milkmaid. Nan Druby was abducted just like you. If Miller is a murderer, is he also the villain who took you?"

Closing her eyes, she tried to force the broken pieces of her memories to return. Nothing, no image became clear. "I don't know. I don't think so."

"This time we have to be sure. No doubts. If he hurt you, so help me, I'll kill him. I don't care if he did save my life."

"Wait. Barrington, just wait." She put her hands to her temples. A prayer or scream for truth and for Barr illuminated in her spirit. She hurt for him. He loved Miller like a brother.

Shutting her lids tight, she let the memories invade. Fear raced her spine as she pictured the trees at the distant part of the Tomàs Orchard. Slap. She struck the canvas with her brush, over and over. Tears had stained her vision. Then it happened, the monster came. He pulled his cape over her eyes, shrouded her in darkness. She had raised her hands high and punched his arm.

Amora opened her eyes and bolted off the stool straight into Barrington's arms. "Not him. My abductor was very tall. One heavy arm grabbed at my neck." Water, unwanted and uncontrollable, drizzled down her cheek. "It was a thick arm, so much so I couldn't breathe."

She swiped the stream away and recalled her anger and her power. "Not a victim any more. No more. I won't be. Monster, you will have a name."

Barrington scooped her up and held her. She shivered. "You're not. You are safe. Say it with me."

She coughed, fighting for air. She shook her head. "Why?"

"Because you need to. I can't let you get so worked up. You could... get sick. Remember, Mrs. Hessing's horrid dinner. I don't want to clean up anything. I'm bone tired tonight from stealing a body and interrogating an unconscious man. No more work for me or poor James."

She let his attempt at humor slow her pulse and savored the feel of his hands along her hips, the small of her back. The scent of him, musky and earthy, fought against her trembles. Well, the ones caused from fright.

Never had she been more aware of him and how good it felt to be cradled against his chest. Her fingertips curled onto the lapels of his open robe.

His gaze searched hers as if something were written upon her pupils. He dipped his head, kissed her brow, then released her. Playing with his sash, he rotated toward his friend. "We still don't know why Miller is alive or how he happened to be in the place your abductor kept you. Could he be in league with the monster? The man I visited the night you *miscarried*, he was hired to help carry out an evil man's crimes, also an abductor."

She put a hand to Barrington's elbow. "I can't see such darkness in Gerald Miller. He'd never aid a fiend."

"I couldn't see him as a deserter either. Things change. People change. I'm not sure of anything anymore."

The ice block shrouding her heart melted even more. He was in such agony over Miller. "We are going to learn the truth, Barr. We are. We'll prove he's not a murderer or anything else untoward."

Her husband's face was bleak. Lines formed in the corners of his frown. "One thing is certain, Miller won't be able to tell us more tonight. My cousin, with his medical knowledge, can help. He'll need to be discrete. If I can't convince him of that, perhaps a client whose neck I've saved from the gallows can."

She clutched at his robe as if holding onto it would keep him safe. "Don't deal with criminals, Barrington. That's too dangerous. I don't want you putting yourself at more risk."

That half-smile appeared again as he took her palm and led her to the door. "I'll be careful. Well, more careful."

Exiting, he nodded to James who leaped from the wall and slogged back into Miller's room. "Come on, Mrs. Norton. It's time for you to rest."

"How can we sleep with so much happening?"

He didn't answer and led her back to the main landing. Shutting the door to the cellar, he shook his head and dropped his gaze to floor. It was as if the house had fallen in upon his shoulders. "If this added strain harms you, I'll never forgive myself. You deserve so much better."

She made him turn and lifted his chin. "If we solve this mystery, you will be giving me the greatest gift. My life back. Maybe I'll see a morning without nightmares. We may even be able to learn Sarah's whereabouts."

His eyes had dulled again. Not quite the level of desperation he had when he was in his office, but very close. "The costs to you, to us, may be very high. Too high, Amora."

"It's too late to turn back. You can't un-steal him. No one will find out Miller is here. James is loyal. We'll find other ways to throw suspicion off of you. You'll still be one of the crown's trusted barristers."

There was something in his expression, the twitch of his cheek that screamed this was bigger than his career. What filled his head? And why did it feel thick and dire?

"My career. Yes, my precious career. It comes before you, doesn't it?"

"I'm sorry. I know that isn't fair. What is it you are not telling me?"

Her pulse raced as she could almost see the gears of truth and consequences turning in his head. He paused and shifted his stance as if weighing the options or excuses. "I'd like to say nothing, but that would be a lie."

How could she hope to be stronger if he held such low expectations of her? Everything inside her winced. She couldn't give up. He needed her and she wouldn't let him fight this alone. "Don't push me away. We can figure this out together."

"We have to find your Sarah more than ever. Your memories and hers have to be enough to puzzle this out. The magistrate gave me two names, Sarah Calloway and Sarah Growlins. Does either sound familiar?"

She rubbed at her temples, but the only thing in her

head was fear for Barrington. "No."

"Both were abducted around the same time as you. The details in their complaints match your horrors."

The twitch in his cheek became more pronounced. Barrington could make his handsome features stone when he needed to win at trial. She'd seen it. What he knew must be horrid, but he needed to tell all. "Say the rest."

"I am more convinced. I fear that you and Sarah and Miller are involved with the Dark Walk Abductor."

She heard his words, but they didn't move her as much as his telling her his fears. Barrington did trust her strength.

Her heart pounded, beating with expectation and joy. Had they moved to such a place in their relationship, that he would always believe in her?

"Time for bed for you, Mrs. Norton. We are going to have a long day tomorrow. For normalcy, I'll head to Lincoln's Inn, but be ready by 5:00. We won't be able to visit Miss Growlins until the evening, that is if her father gives permission."

She nodded. He led her back upstairs, all the way to her room. "We are solving this together. I'll be ready."

Slowly, he pushed open her door then stood in the threshold to prevent her from entering. "I apologize again for bringing this to Mayfair. Don't go down to see Miller. He's not the man we remember from Clanville. He could be a murderer or worse. I'm going to have James find someone to watch him during the day."

Her fingers soaked up the warmth of his palm. "Mother knows herbs. She could help Mr. Miller. That would limit the number of people who know."

"No. The pharaoh can't know of this. Our truce will

be done. Yet, what accusation of hers wouldn't be true? I've endangered you all." He pressed his lips together so tightly they seemed like pages of a closed book.

Why had she been so blind to see that he cared for family as much as his career?

A noisy sigh left him. "Beakes is no fool. He might've bought our little theater tonight, but he'll be watching the house, you and me, to see if we can lead him to Miller."

He took their linked hands and tapped them against his chest. Try to avoid telling Mrs. Tomàs."

"I make no promises on keeping secrets from you or her."

His head bobbed. "Good policy." He put his hands about her waist. His thumbs massaged her middle again. I need for you to believe in me, too. My desire for us to be happy, to be united has not changed."

Her breath stuck as she tried to think of reasons against this notion. It was difficult with the press of his fingers drawing her closer. Could she give in to the pull, the whirlwind of loving him, of being loved by him?

She swallowed and looked away from his hungry silver eyes.

Barrington sighed low, like a tiger's growl. He moved his palms. "Let's see what we can uncover these final seven days of our bargain. Pity we can't find reasons to extend your stay."

He took her hand and put it to his jaw. The slight stubble made her fingers vibrate. "Do you know of any reasons why you should stay longer, Amora? Ones strong enough to forget this separating business?"

"I can't think of leaving you now. Not with all the risk."

"What of when this is over? For I will find the villain. What about then?"

If she said yes, would things go as well as the last time she let her whole heart love him? "I don't want to think too far ahead. Things change and never for the better."

He pushed at his brow. "Then we'll think about now, one day or night at a time."

Amora focused on his silvery smoky eyes. Her fingers danced across the firm muscles of his bared chest before she pulled away. The need to lie safe within his arms made her skin tingle, but she couldn't. She wasn't strong enough to weather disappointing him again. "Goodnight."

She spun to her door. He held onto her hand. Like the turn of a waltz, he swirled her to him. The heat in his gaze, the curve of his lip set her heart a flutter. She didn't want to be alone. Nightmares awaited her when she slept.

He bent his head and took her lips. His hands went under her robe, caressing her. His fingers sculpted her against him.

Losing herself with him, would it be so wrong?

All her intentions of leaving him outside of her chambers disappeared as he planted kisses at the base of her neck.

"Tell me yes, Amora."

Consent was on her tongue. Couldn't he taste it?

Did she have to admit to needing him aloud?

One arm went about his waist. The other stubbornly stayed still.

She let him have his way with her mouth. Her robe slipped, offering a shoulder for his hands to claim. Surrendering to his strength seemed right.

His kisses deepened. They became more demanding, but he hadn't taken her shoulder or lifted her fully into his arms. He wanted her to choose.

"One delicious word, that's what I want. What is your desire?"

On tiptoes, she leaned up to keep his retreating lips. The feel of his heated breath falling upon her cheek brought more words than yes. It returned I miss you. I need you. 1 love you. Words she'd locked away in the pit of her soul.

Cold air met her shivering form. Her skin pimpled as he moved away. His passion for her ended with him retying his robe. "Stubborn, like the Pharaoh. Aye, Amora?"

She blinked a dozen times only to witness her husband heading to the stairs. "Barrington?"

He stopped and half-turned, straightening his lapel. "I think I'll wait for the woman who confronted me in my study tonight. The one who knows, without a doubt, what she wants."

"She may not exist. It's hard not to have doubts when it comes to us."

"Never doubt that I want you. Don't guess at my heart. I'd rather spend another frustrated night at Mayfair, than having you regret loving me, hating the miracle and consequences of being in my arms." He leaned against the wall and released a deep moan. "Five o'clock tomorrow. We'll go talk to Sarah Growlins. As a matter of fact, be out of the house. Go to Cheapside with Mrs. Tomàs for upholstery or your orphanage with the housekeeper. At five, we'll meet here. If Mr. Growlins hasn't answered, we'll go to a play and not one of Miss Miller's."

She almost chuckled. Barr had finally seen her duplicity. "The vicar's taking us on a family outing to a park."

His lips thinned again. "Fine, play family with him. Just be away from Miller. Give the Norton's the appearance of normalcy, whatever that is."

As his footsteps thudded farther away, she slipped into her room, shut the door and let her pulse slow to a crawl. Alone. All alone, she flopped into her bed, wrinkling the empty sheets. With her skin humming, smelling of Barrington, it wouldn't be nightmares awaiting her tonight.

That scared her heart more than anything.

Chapter Three: Secret Pregnancy, Maybe

Barrington pounded into his office at the Lincoln's Inn and slammed into his chair. He couldn't concentrate in the Old Bailey. He knocked over briefs and narrowly won an easy trial. How could his mind work properly? The last twenty-four hours changed everything. His dead best friend was alive and possibly a murderer or worse the Dark Walk Abductor.

And Amora was pregnant. She carried Barrington's child in her womb and still wanted to separate.

He scratched his forehead as he counted the months since the last time they made love. Goodness. Three, almost four months ago before all the madness. She's with child! His child!

His heart flipped with pure joy then dropped down to the recesses of his gut. She only wanted to stay past their separation deadline because of Miller, nothing else.

If she was pregnant, why wasn't she aware? Something living on the inside, gaining life, growing... Wouldn't a woman notice? Maybe he was leaping to the conclusions he wanted to be true. What were the facts?

He tapped his quill, took a cut of foolscap and started to pen his brief.

The nausea. Just like before, Amora spent most of the days dizzy, vomiting. Check.

The sensitivity to smells. Just like before, strong smells like coffee or flowers made her feel wretched. Check.

The changes to her body. The feel of her in his arms last night, hadn't there been more to cup, more than her normal curves? But she hadn't gained as much weight as she had last time.

Well, of course she hadn't. He wasn't feeding her sweet ice from Gunter's to settle her stomach.

He held his paper up. If he were Justice Burns, he'd put on his dark cap to pronounce judgment. Amora Norton was guilty of carrying his child. She should be sentenced to a lifetime of loving him. Pity, the woman wanted an appeal.

Even with kisses that would test the resolve of a monk, she hadn't refused to separate. Yet, how strong would her resistance last given the fire arching betwixt them?

And if she gave in, what would make things different this time? The strain on her wasn't any less. If denying needing Barrington gave her strength, how could he wish her to surrender?

He groaned aloud. Taking the jewel case from his pocket, he smoothed the velvet nape within his palm. He thought of giving her his modified present at breakfast, one he'd worked on through the night, sort of a reward for saving him, but she and the Pharaoh had been caught up in discussions of their big outing with the vicar.

The convenient vicar. What did they truly know of him?

If Beakes wasn't so busy trying to prove Barrington guilty, he'd have him investigating Wilson.

Yet, Amora smiled and even laughed this morning. She hadn't been this at ease in Mayfair since there return from Clanville.

He even got in a quick kiss when she came to his office before he left for court. How could he disrupt the Pharaoh's apple cart by giving Amora his present, another bauble as she'd put it, that might remind her of all his mistakes.

With a shove, he stuffed the jewel into his coat pocket. This token wouldn't keep her smiles.

Avoiding the temptation of banging his head against the waxed writing surface, he slouched deeper into his chair.

Amora was so strong last night. Her quick thinking saved him, keeping him out of Newgate. She didn't crumble seeing Miller. The woman wanted to be at his side to find Sarah. How long would she remain confident and sound in her reasoning?

Harboring these secrets may have kept her womb shuttered, making it so difficult to be with child. Last year, the strain of the memories caused her to miscarry. What about this time?

His head smacked against the desk, taking most of his vigor. *God, what do I do now to save Amora?*

Oh, was there a way to undo this promise of taking Amora to Sarah Growlins tonight? With Amora in a delicate condition, she had to be more vulnerable. Sarah's father hadn't written back his permission for a visit. Perhaps Mr. Growlins's delay was an unexpected blessing.

From the records, Miss Growlins was not only an

abduction victim. From all accounts taken from that lone stretch of trees, the Dark Walk in Vaux Hall, Growlins was a victim of the great fiend. If this woman is his Amora's Sarah, then only one question remained. Was Miller the fiend?

If her Sarah was in a bad state, that would hurt Amora. This hunt would take a toll. The strain had to be twice, no three times the strain as bad as keeping these horrible secrets. Their child would have no chance.

Having not heard from God, well, not hearing the answers he wanted, Barrington had let his worship grow cold. Perhaps this was the kick he needed to make it burn more brightly. He yanked his Bible from the bottom of the pile of case law books on his desk. Running his fingers through the leaves, he happened upon King David fasting and praying for his first child with Bathsheba.

King David wept and cried aloud for mercy. But, none of the coercions forced the Lord's hand. Their child still died.

Barrington's heart shuddered. "Lord, I'm a humble beggar with no promises to make. Nothing to persuade You, Lord. But I will still ask. I will still beg. Give us the chance to see our child breathe."

Barrington let his shoulder's droop. All the tired, sleepy air releasing from his lungs, vibrated his lips. He'd sat up with his new house guest all night, giving James much needed rest. Poor Miller was a shell. His body quaked throughout the night.

Barrington had seen the quivers before in a pick-pocket from the Rookery and a high-borne thief in Grosvenor. Miller might be like them, addicted to opium, Dover pills as they were known.

Though quiet and dazed when Barrington first took him, Miller's fits grew worse with each passing hour. How had he continued to get the drugs unless the doctors at Bedlam fed them to him?

Too many questions.

Barrington sat up and pushed at his brow, hoping to drive out the headache settling into his skull.

The knock upon his door made him flinch.

"Sir, there is a woman here." One of the inn's clerks, with the wits to know not to barge inside, rapped the door again. "Sir, she insists Mrs. Norton sent her to you."

Did Amora find her Sarah? Was the woman out searching for her friend on her own or with the ever helpful vicar? He wiped his mouth of jealousy and arose. "Just a moment."

He leaned over and clenched the chiseled curves of the desk. Amora was determined to put herself in danger. Why must she temp fate? Leaping out of a carriage the night she'd miscarried, standing on a cliff in the midst of a storm. Why did she court these dangers?

Did she think about the consequences to the baby?

Or worse. What if she didn't want *his* babe?

A cold sweat damped his lip. He tugged on his waistcoat and moved forward, refusing to surrender to despair. Their love, however imbalanced, would make it somehow and so would this child. He stuffed a prayer for her deep inside his gut and opened the door.

The clerk stepped backward and exposed Cynthia Miller.

Barrington winced again as the liar entered. "Oh, it's you, Miss Miller."

The clerk craned his neck, glaring at them until the door closed.

Chrysanthemum fragrance filled his office as Cynthia untied her cape and let it slip to a chair. "Is that what it takes to see the busy barrister, offering Amora's name?"

Dressed in clinging brown, maybe red, she pranced about his drab office.

Displaying her womanly curves and a wide smile, she spun close to his bookcase poking at the spines. "Mr. Norton, I'm desperate. My brother is missing. You must help me find him."

He leaned against the door framing and pulled his sore arms across his chest. "This missing brother is the one you allowed the world to believe is dead, five years dead."

She blinked at him, her lips pouting. "You know him to be alive. You've seen him, haven't you?"

"I admit to nothing. I just want to know why you would hide someone you believe to be your brother away from friends and family?"

She moved near. Gloveless, her forward hands gripped the lapel of his tailcoat. Her naked fingers appeared so light against his coal colored coat. "Do you know where he is?"

"Perhaps I'll tell you in five years." Swatting free, he held the door open. "Good day, Miss Miller."

She shoved it closed and laid against it. "I should've told you. I just didn't know how."

He moved back to his desk, his blood churning with her deceit. His world of seeing almost no color collapsed upon her, painting her black with guilty. "You've bent my ear over music, your premieres. Goodness knows how many errands I've done because you had no brother to help. Yet, you couldn't tell me something so fundamental."

With a shrug, she opened her mouth, then closed it quickly. At least a minute passed before her lyrical voice sounded. "I... I thought I could manage things."

"Does that include drugging said man and keeping him locked away in a private area of Bedlam?"

"Drugging?" Her cheeks darkened. "I'd never harm him."

"Well, maybe the person helping you fund the care of this mystery man has fed him opium or the like to keep him in a stupor. Why?"

She sank to the floor in a puddle, heaving. "I'd never hurt Gerald, never. You must believe me."

Tears drizzled down Cynthia's face. "Don't hate me. I can't stand you hating me."

Barrington sighed and dropped his arms to his sides. He didn't like lies. Maybe he'd frightened Cynthia with his reaction, just as he had Amora. Tugging a handkerchief from his tailcoat, he slogged over and handed the linen to her. "Gerald is safe. Ask no more questions. With all you've had to deal with, I can understand your reticence, I suppose."

"Don't pity me." She seized his arm and pulled against his chest. "I'm not the pitying sort." She weaved her arms beneath his waistcoat and kissed his cheek. "I'm the sort to adore."

He pried at the iron grip of her fingers. "What are you doing?"

With a wave of her hand, she undid his cravat. "Finally showing you the woman I am."

She took his lips before he could pull away. The offering was tart, buttered with more lies.

He stepped away from her and wiped at his mouth. "You belong to Bedlam if you think I'd break my vows."

"Wouldn't you rather be with someone who loves you as you are - tall, dark, and handsome? No changes required."

His brow rose. "What?"

"You've changed your schedule because of Amora. You see people you think she'd approve of. You've avoided me since your return from Clanville. She's remaking you, but why ruin perfection?"

Wasn't modifying his ways what he needed to do to secure his wife's affections? Yet, it hadn't quite worked. She hadn't chosen him, just the mystery. He lowered his gaze to the notched boards of the floor. Maybe hope was there.

Cynthia traipsed close and put her hands on his ruined neckcloth. "Hadn't you complained to me how you'd wished to attend my events, but Amora didn't feel well? She uses everything to keep you under her thumb. You don't want to be enslaved to her like old Mr. Tomàs was to her mother."

He backed away, moving near his bookcase. Maybe he'd shared his marital difficulties once too often with Cynthia. Couldn't one woman shed light upon what another thought?

And no, he wasn't going to be ruled by a pharaoh.

Cynthia traipsed into his shadow again. Her warm palm rubbed his tired shoulders, massaged the tension in his back. "When is she considerate of your needs? From the knots in your neck, it's been a long time."

"Cynthia, Miss Miller? You need to leave. It's not proper for you to be here saying such things."

"I haven't been proper for a long time." She blew a wet kiss in his ear. "And Amora gave her permission."

He pivoted. "For what?"

Cynthia leaned into him on tiptoes. "To be your mistress."

Searching Cynthia's pretty countenance, he saw nothing but hardness and a triumphant shrewdness. Where was the kind woman he believed was his friend?

He seized her elbows and gave her a light shake. "Is this the face Amora witnesses, a woman bound to harlot herself with a married man?"

Cynthia recoiled and moved well out of his reach. Her breath came in huffs. "Haven't I waited long enough? You do want me, Barrington. I know you do. And she doesn't. Not anymore."

His fist hit the bookcase before he could stop it. He couldn't surrender to Cynthia's lies. Amora just needed more time. "Get out of my office."

"I just saw her getting on a boat ride to Vaux Hall. She looked quite happy. She wasn't thinking of you."

"Vaux Hall?" He felt his temper slipping from his control. "She went there alone?"

"Not alone. She looked content with Vicar Wilson's arm about her."

Amora. Had she chosen Wilson? Did any of her kisses last night mean anything? No. Hope was dead.

Cynthia stepped closer. She rubbed his forearm. "If you'd chosen me before you left for the Peninsula, you'd have a wife who worships you and a daughter, maybe more children."

His heart twisted until it broke, this time for good. He had no wife that adored him. They'd lost their first child and had no guarantees the second would survive. All he had was a name that needed to be kept respectable and a minister that needed to be bludgeoned.

He thumbed his brow. "Stay here if you must. I'm

going to retrieve my wife."

Barrington reached behind the door and grabbed his top hat.

"Please, Barrington. Wait." Her high pitched pleas made his pace quicken.

"Good day, Miss Miller."

He swung open the door and watched Hessing pop up as if he'd been watching through the keyhole.

"Uh, Norton," his mentor said, "I need you to join me for supper at my club tonight."

Socializing when he needed to retrieve his wife from Wilson? He shook his head. "I'm very busy. This isn't a good time. Miss Miller, you must leave, now."

She scooped her cape. "When you come to your senses," she tossed the dark fabric about her shoulders, "you know where to find me."

She held her head up and swept out of his office.

Hessing smothered a chuckle. He seemed to enjoy watching Cynthia slink to the stairs. "Breaking with a mistress can be tough, Norton."

"She's not..." He held his tongue. No use explaining. Any nugget fed the gossiping beast and Hessing would use it to his advantage in court. "Was there something you needed, sir?"

"There are always other flowers, Norton. Don't be so glum. We need to speak of your career."

"Another time, sir. I've—"

"Mr. Beakes is joining me too, with much to discuss. I would hate for you to be caught up in something to appease or quiet a mistress, Norton. You've done very well, but it can all be gone with a blink. As much as I would like to help, I'll have no influence on the matter."

The glare in Hessing's eyes spoke volumes. The safety

of being Hessing's project, the favored mulatto, would end if the man felt Barrington was duplicitous.

Warning heeded, he nodded his head. "I have a few errands, sir. But, I'll be there."

He jammed on his hat and left his mentor. His heart pounded, matching his footfalls upon the steps. He didn't dare look back and show Hessing hesitation. The fellow didn't need to witness the angst building. For he might wrongly assume the apprehension to be over the ill-fated dinner invitation. In reality, Barrington had finally accepted the loss of Amora's love. Perhaps that was why God had been silent.

Lunging into his carriage, he let his aches reign for his arms, his pride, his dreams, everything stung. He'd go retrieve Amora, not as a husband desperate to persuade his wife for another chance. But, as man fighting for his child. If it meant saving the life of his babe, he'd turn in Miller and let Amora go.

Chapter Four: An Outing to Vaux Hall

The vicar's outing or diversion as Amora thought of it, began with a short boat ride across the breezy Thames to arrive at the crowded Vaux Hall Gardens.

The noise hit her first, loud and joyful. Then the fresh, sweet scent of river water mixed with cooked meats. So much for a morning without nausea.

Samuel bounced his son in his arms as he waved to a smiling Rebecca and a very cheery Mama. The two headed toward a throng of people where music, jaunty tunes with wild beats, seemed to emanate.

The man smiled and held out his arm, "Shall we venture forward, Mrs. Norton?"

With the noises, the smells, and more boat loads of people arriving to Vaux Hall, it was probably best to delve deeper into the park.

"Thank you, Vicar, for arranging this today. I think I needed a distraction from Mayfair."

His brow scrunched. "I've never been called a distraction before. But, let's see what we can do about being helpful."

She adjusted the ribbons of her straw bonnet and took his elbow. She tried to appear at ease and unhurried. Ignoring her churning stomach, she lifted her head. The budding greenery might help alleviate her angst.

"If we are moving too fast, I can slow down. With all of Jackson's squirming, I might be going too fast for his enjoyment as well."

The boy did squirm a bit. His creamy white pinafore whipped back and forth against Samuel's dark charcoal coat.

"I might be impatient, too. Mr. Norton, may have found a lost friend of mine. I hope it is her. I was very disappointed the last time."

The sadness of the last Sarah had made everything hurt. The depression of it lasted longer than it should have. Barrington was right to be concerned. "Yes, very sad."

Samuel shook his head and continued up the path stopping near a flutist. The tune was simple. Bliss bounced in the chords.

But it didn't bounce inside Amora. She'd gone to Barrington's study this morning to remind herself of all that had transpired. Helping him, seeing Mr. Miller couldn't be another curious dream. Moreover, her very protective husband could've changed his mind, refusing to take her to visit the newly found Sarahs.

What began as a small morning goodbye kiss between her and Barrington as co-conspirators, ended with his palms on her abdomen. The same motion he always did when she was with child.

For him, it might just be a habit. But, the feeling and the pressure had for the first time felt familiar.

Mama was right.

It wasn't Mrs. Hessing's dinner that made her ill.

It wasn't weakness from falling or anything else. It was the new life inside her.

She shook her head to the irony.

Samuel leaned his head toward her. His careful walnut eyes raked over her, probably assessing her spirit. But, no one could tell the dance fear and happiness did in her womb.

"Yes, Vicar?"

He bit his lip for a moment then turned toward the stands. "I don't think we'll see a tight-rope walker today. My bishop says the park is still a bit subdued. This full mourning, half-mourning business."

"Maybe we should leave, sir."

"It's Samuel, remember? And we have just arrived. Look at how your mother and Rebecca have scouted off, all smiles. Let's endure a little longer for them."

Needing something for her fidgeting fingers to do she reached up and took the vicar's son into her arms. Holding a baby had new meaning today. "Yes, a little longer. I wasn't thinking of them."

"Your mind does seem to be far away." He led her a little farther passed the noisy crowds closer to the lush hedgerows. "I take it you and Mr. Norton are still having disagreements?"

Hackles raised, she stopped and turned to face him.

Samuel's countenance was earnest. Nothing like Cynthia's, hoping for an advantage. "Vicar, you are a dear man. But—"

"I didn't mean to pry. I'm just hoping you two will reconcile." He started to chuckle as he leveled his domed hat. "I do see more of Mrs. Tomàs in you some days, more than others."

She shook her head to him and tried to right the squirming Jackson within her arms. "Well, Mother has some wonderful traits. This young boy takes after you, always so lively." She half-pivoted and took a breath as the boy made a soft kick against her stomach. "I'd like to rest."

The vicar pointed to a bench in the distance. "I suppose he wants to see everything. For me, that includes happy couples."

He nodded and held out his palm. "There seems to be benches this way. Let's head to them."

After shifting Jackson to the other side, she took the vicar's arm.

He made more small talk and oohs and ahs of the juggler they passed. None of this mattered to Amora. As amiable as Samuel was, he wasn't the man whose ears she needed to bend.

Patting little Jackson's back, she took a big whiff of his lavender scented blanket. It softened the oily aroma of the roasted meats strewn about their path and gave her stomach a needed respite.

Plopping on to the bench, she settled Jackson, then cupped her stomach to smooth the deep, dark blue fabric of her carriage gown. Yes, cupping her stomach, just as Barrington did.

There was no more denying or ignoring the signs. Only two things remained unsettled. How would Barrington respond? And more importantly, would she be able to carry the child to term?

Her abdomen quivered as fear settled again like a hard lump to her middle. Well, next to the small lump of life.

Samuel sat beside her. "This will give you a great view

of everything. The perfect place to rest."

"I think you are right."

The tree line framing their position in Vaux Hall made it wonderful, so much green like Tomàs land. Emerald blades of new grass, leaves of jade surrounding new buds in the trees. All so beautiful and lively, all contrasting the people wandering around in mourning grabs of gray and black.

Samuel stretched out and started to hum. His head pitched to and fro. Perhaps the sights and sounds were too much for this country vicar. "My bishop said this was a good place to venture, but to watch the meat. I wonder what that means."

Stomach roiling over the word meat, she lifted the wiggling Jackson to him. "Here, Vicar. Take your son. I think he wants his father."

Samuel hefted the boy in the air and flopped him onto his lap. The spry thing stilled and began jiggling the vicar's darkened buttons. "Spring colds are the worse. So is that your ailment or did something happen at the Hessing's party to drain your zeal? That Miller woman looked as if she could be bothersome."

Again with more questions. The man was persistent. She rotated from father and son and scanned the walking path behind the bench with her gaze. "I'm fine," she said in her most convincing voice.

When she spun back, his forehead crinkled. His walnut colored eyes clouded. "If you say so."

She should tell him that this wasn't a cold or a lingering weakness from nearly drowning. But it was Barrington's right to know this matter first. How would she tell her husband?

And what did it all mean for them?

She needed to not be under anyone's scrutiny. "Vicar, go show this wiggly worm the sights."

"You want to be alone? Are you sure?"

Cold sweat dotted her brow, but she brushed it away. "Yes, I'll be fine here in the sunshine."

Samuel shrugged, then stood. "Yes, being in the light and filled with it, is the best." He hefted his boy upon his shoulder and headed straight for the crowds. "I won't be far away."

She watched father and son head down the smallish hill.

Alone, she hugged her arms and let her mind be free to fret. Barrington was in such trouble. If Beakes could prove Barrington stole Miller, he would be jailed. Now, in the midst of this and their hunt for Sarah, Amora and Barrington had a baby to think of. So many things could go wrong. Babies were fragile, and they needed a good mother. How could that be her? Wasn't she just as fragile?

Barrington said he desired the confident woman who saved him last night. She wanted to be that woman too, always, not just in fleeting moments.

She looked down at her trembling fingers, the ones numbering potential catastrophe. How can she hold onto her strength and still fear the dark? How could she both hope and dread her returning memories? When would she no longer think like a victim and have victory over the past?

The wind shifted, prickling her skin. The sound of crunching leaves, the noise of footfalls came nearer. She turned her head to the trees.

A lone figure, large and thick moved toward her. The shadow of the branches lifted from his damaged countenance. Lord Clanville, Mr. Charleton's brother, approached. He tugged his onyx eye patch and quickened his steps, arriving in three long strides to the rear of her bench.

He twisted to one side, obscuring the burnt part of his face. "Miss Tomàs, what are you doing in L-London?" His speech was slow with a lisp. "You l-left Clanville without a word, years ago. The l-last time I saw you."

What was best way to answer without exposing herself to rumors or pity? "Barrington Norton is my betrothed, my husband. We have a residence here."

"Norton." His jaw worked hard as if it took an effort to pronounce Barrington's surname.

Why did she need to defend her marriage to the Charleton family? They were very rich, but the Norton and Tomàs clans were not in want of means of connections. Barrington's inheritance alone made him quite well off, though he hated drawing upon it.

Was it because Barrington was a mulatto?

It didn't matter to her. It shouldn't matter to others. Lord Clanville had no right thinking of how others looked with his own deficiencies.

"Him."

She shrugged her shoulders. Men and their stupid games.

The man lumbered closer. His height towered over her as if he inspected the pleating of her carriage dress for a flaw.

Impeccable in shimmering dark blue, it was one of the ensembles her mother procured. She didn't feel miserable wearing this slight bit of color during this time of mourning.

"Norton, the barrister, took you?" His lone exposed

eye, dark jade like Rebecca's, squinted at her before the earl raised his head toward the trees. "'Cept for last night, I haven't seen you out to gatherings."

He was at Hessing's ball? Maybe he'd become shy because of his injuries. She slipped her fingers into a steeple. "I didn't see you, but I suppose neither of us care much for socializing."

"One of the many things I t-treasured of our acquaintance."

She pivoted on the bench inching away from the earl. There was never partiality on her side. "I don't understand."

The blankness of this half of his uncovered face, no smile or frown, set a shiver down her spine. She swiveled to locate Samuel or Mama.

It didn't need to be dark to make her feel trapped. A hint of his salve on his face twisted her stomach. "My party will be back soon."

He turned his full face towards her and stared. "Good. No one should be alone."

Pity a reckless carriage fire stole his handsome features and most of his nose.

A sigh left him as he pivoted and lumbered down the path he'd come.

When his tailcoat could no longer be seen, she breathed out the building irritation from her lungs and sunk into the bench, setting her gaze to the revelers in Vaux Hall. From a distance, she could see a man swinging a girl high. Could it be the vicar and Rebecca? Maybe a vision of Amora with Papa.

The music faded in the gentle breeze. She closed her eyes. A wave of oaks and Pippen apple trees swayed about her.

A paintbrush had lodged between her fingers. Slapping at a canvas with anger and oils, she witnessed the colors take shape.

A hand snatched her shoulder.

Her breath got stuck in her throat. She tried to cry out but couldn't. Swinging and hitting at the arm didn't prevent her from being picked up. A blurred view of a face hovered above before cloth shrouded her eyes.

She grunted, balled her fist and punched the air. No more a victim. She struck the air again and again.

Something blunted her third blow.

"Amora! Amora."

Not again.

Large hands took her wrists, but she continued to struggle. She wouldn't be taken. Not again, not alive.

"Wake up, Amora. It's Barrington."

She batted her lids and focused on the cleft in his chin. "Barr?"

He released her, then smoothed a tendril from her cheek. With both hands cradling her jaw, he sat and edged closer. "Is this how the vicar lets you spend the afternoon? Alone and unprotected?"

Not caring about the censure in his voice, she leaned into her husband, burying herself within his embrace. Only after hearing three hundred and twelve heartbeats did she move. She sat erect. Her nose wrinkled. Chrysanthemum stench. "I see Miss Miller's been to see you."

He folded his arms as his full lips pressed into a deeper line. "So you can have male friends, and I receive condemnation for my female friends?"

"Vicar Wilson has no intentions of seducing me."

Barrington's brow rose. His dark cheeks looked

strained. "I'm not giving anyone permission to tempt you." The temperature of his breath chilled against her skin. "But Miss Miller said you did. Did she lie? Did you give the woman permission to seduce me?"

She looked down at his dark button of his deep gray waistcoat and nodded. "She angered me at Hessing's party. I told her to try."

"Why? Why would you do that to me? You think nothing of my commitment? Hessing saw her at my office. He and the whole Lincoln's Inn thinks she's my mistress."

"She loves you, Barrington. And she's pretty and sane. Sometimes, I think you should've married her."

Barrington seemed on the verge of exploding. Even worse than last night, her husband's veneer of calm appeared permanently severed. "I am married in case you've forgotten. We haven't signed any separation agreement, not that a piece of paper would make any liaison with Cynthia Miller right. I think you want me to be an adulterer like my father. Will that ease your guilt for allowing another man to raise my child?"

She blinked at him. He thought her pregnant, too.

He stashed his gloves into his pocket, reached out and caressed her stomach. He drew small rings around her abdomen just as he did before, when he celebrated the life within her. "My child. That one night before everything went awry gave us another miracle."

She covered his hand, keeping it upon her abdomen. "I don't know what to say."

"You weren't going to tell me at all?" His voice grew small, slowed. "You would willingly keep this secret from me?"

The aroma of putrid flowers in his jacket made her

head light. "I wouldn't hide my pregnancy. I'd tell you when I was sure, but you reek."

He pulled her closer. "Enjoy. It's the present you sent to my office. Some men only get slippers. Such a thoughtful wife."

"You were with Cynthia?"

"Isn't that what you wanted for me? To have me drown in her forwardness and then come back repentant to you. More chits to hold over my head."

Though her heart raced from his caress, the notion of him touching Cynthia, kissing Cynthia turned her stomach. She leapt from the bench and squinted at him. "You didn't bed her. You're not like that. Barrington Norton is honorable."

He folded his arms and rubbed his chin. The silence between them lasted more than a minute. Each moment squeezed her heart, more and more.

Finally, his lips parted. "I have not been unfaithful, Amora. Though the whole of Lincoln's Inn thinks otherwise." He rubbed his brow. The emotion in his voice was so thick, the sorrow-filled weight crushed her soul. "I might be a dull barrister, but even I can understand a woman who's changed her mind about loving me. I finally understand."

The collar to her coat seemed choking. "What are you saying?"

Mama and Samuel, with the vicar's children in tow, traipsed closer. Happy, noisy banter enrobed them.

Barrington lifted his head. He stared at the vicar. "You may not love me, Amora, but I'll fight for this child. I have rights."

"Mr. Norton, you've come to join us." Mama lifted a piece of roast lamb from her bun. "See how thin it's cut."

Samuel turned his head betwixt Amora and Barrington. "Is everything well?"

Her husband charged at her friend. "Why on earth would you bring my wife here?"

Samuel put his son in Mama's arms. "Mrs. Norton said you agreed that we could go on an outing."

Though Samuel might be able to handle himself, Barrington seemed out of control. For the first time ever, Amora was frightened at what he would do to the vicar.

"Mama, take the children back to the festival."

She shook her head as she pulled Rebecca into her dark skirts. "I'm not leaving you or Vicar Wilson."

"Please, Mama. All will be well."

Wilson patted her hand as he took off his top hat and fanned. "Henutsen, it's fine. I'll catch up with you in a moment."

She shook her head, took the children and traipsed back toward the crowds.

"Now. Where were we?" Barrington said as he stormed within a foot of the vicar. "Yes, you are going to explain why you brought my wife so close to the Dark Walk?" He grabbed Samuel by the elbow and dragged him nearer the bench pointing to the distant grove. "The Dark Walk is through those trees. That's where all those women were stolen. That's where you stole those women."

Barrington raised his arm as if to strike Samuel.

Amora ran and took hold of her husband's arm. "Don't. It's not him. He'd never hurt me."

Her friend broke free. His face paled. "I didn't know, Norton. I just heard it was a green park with music. I'd never put your wife in harm."

Barrington charged again at Samuel, but Amora hung

onto his arm. He stopped and released a long, ragged breath. He sounded like a dragon wheezing. "Why are you in our lives, Wilson? There's more to this than being a Good Samaritan. If you are not the fiend, then you must be in league with him."

Samuel stepped back, flipped off his top hat and fanned his face again. "It was happenstance that I was playing cards with the doctor the night of Mrs. Norton's miscarriage. But when I heard her fevered ramblings..." His fingers tightened along the brim of his dome. His voice lowered and then dropped in speed. "I'd heard them...before. I had to help."

Amora latched onto Barrington's elbow. "He's a good man. You know that."

Barrington's jaw twitched. He tugged at his waistcoat causing his buttons to jingle and clap. "I don't know anything anymore. To take you here, of all places, is beyond the pale."

Samuel squared his shoulders and moved very close to him. "I am not he, the man who has taken so much from so many. I came to help. I will stay unless you tell me the work is finished."

He sucked in a deep breath, easing his grimace. He seemed more in control. "Then come with me, Vicar, to meet with Miss Sarah Growlins. We can all take the next boat, then send the ladies to Mayfair in your carriage."

Amora gazed into his furious gray eyes and squeezed his bicep. "I'm to go with you. You promised."

Barrington shook his head. "You will be home resting, madam."

"What of our bargain? I am to help find Sarah." She reached for his cheek, but he stepped away as if her fingertips held poison.

"All commitments need to be re-evaluated. I need to know what I want, what I'm willing to do. Come along, sir."

The vicar moved between them. "Neither of you can see Sarah Growlins. Not today or ever in this life. She's dead."

Amora's ears hurt. She eased backward until the bench pressed against her legs. "She's dead."

Barrington wrenched at his deflated cravat. "You knew that one too."

"Before she was abducted, I was told she was a lively brunette with a great talent for the harp. The Dark Walk Abductor took her joy of music... well, her joy for everything."

"The Dark Walk Abductor." Amora found it hard to breathe. She'd heard of his cruelty in a joke at one of the parties Barrington had her attend. It wasn't funny, then or now. "Barrington, why are you trying to find my Sarah among those victims?"

The look on his face, the twitching cheek as his frown drew into a dot, made her feet numb.

She mouthed the words Dark Walk Abductor several times before her voice caught up. "Dark Walk Abductor? No. You can't think that I was taken by him."

She gazed up at Barrington hoping he would refute it. He said nothing.

When he finally nodded, she started to sway. Her head felt so light.

Barrington caught her and eased her back to the bench. "Yes, Amora. Yes, I'm almost positive."

Anger battled the shock trembling her bosom. She pointed a finger at Samuel. "And you suspected this, too?"

Samuel bowed his head. He kicked a rock with his shoe. "Reverend Playfair sent me to their families, after I helped his sister-in-law overcome the hurt of such an attack. Abduction is the worse type of crime for a woman and her family. Even more so for the Dark Walk Abductor victims. His cruelty knew no bounds."

Amora held in her sobs for this lost Sarah, gripping her middle. In her head, she repeated Dark Walk Abductor, brunette, victim. She rubbed her temples hard. She couldn't be a victim any more. "My Sarah was blonde, but she's probably dead too. Sarah Calloway, the other Sarah on Mr. Norton's list, did you help her?"

Samuel shook his head. "I didn't get the chance. After Miss Growlin's death, Mr. Calloway, her father put her away not knowing how else to help. I had been too timid in helping Miss Growlins. I didn't push when I should have. She never accepted that these crimes were not her fault. This man, the Dark Walk Abductor is pure evil, and his doings are not a deserved punishment to the women for trying to meet with a sweetheart, an innocent flirtation, wearing the wrong dress, or even being angry with God. None of that warrants this evil."

Barrington looked up toward the sky. Was he praying or mumbling like an asylum inmate who'd been pushed to the edge. He lowered his head and gripped his chin. "Where is Miss Calloway?"

Samuel marched closer. His countenance was grim, very dark. "Miss Sarah Calloway is very much alive. The lady does have light colored locks, but she's in Bedlam."

Barrington dropped his face into his palm. "Bedlam."

The groan leaving her husband sounded as if his innards had been twisted into a knot.

Shoulders dragging, he turned back to Amora.

"You've had enough activity for today. I'm taking you home. Vicar, I'll leave you to collect Mrs. Tomàs."

"You do know that I am here to help, Mr. Norton."

A bemused smirk filled Barrington's countenance. "Yes, as much as I am assured of my wife's love. For now, you are welcome in the Norton home. Don't give me a reason to doubt you."

Her heart shuddered at Barrington's warning. Fire filled each tight word.

He held out his arm to her. "Let's go to Mayfair."

Garnering her strength, she raised up and took it, all the while looking at the lone grove of trees. She had a feeling this wouldn't leave her mind.

Samuel blocked their path. "Mr. Norton, I am not an enemy. I love this family and will fight for it, too."

Barrington nodded. The stern expression on his face, the tautness of the forearm muscles beneath his tailcoat seemed as if he hoped for a reason to fight. "Wilson, you may not be a deadly enemy, but a lot of things don't appear lethal until they strike."

The vicar frowned. "I'll get Mr. Calloway's permission to visit with his daughter."

Barrington didn't seem to be listening. His gaze, his glare stayed focused on Amora.

And she felt small and guilty within it.

After a silent boat ride, she wobbled at her husband's side all the way to his awaiting carriage. After a brief word to James, Barrington lifted her inside. The door shut. He looked like a polished bronzed statue, not moving and perhaps not feeling anything for her but anger.

"I was wrong to set Cynthia Miller on you, Barrington."

He swiveled his head to the window without responding. For at least an hour, they sat in silence.

No sharing of the same bench.

No extra caresses.

No jokes.

He was stiff and quiet. The distance betwixt them seemed like miles. Her heart quivered. Maybe even her tummy too. For the first time in a long time, she felt someone else's pain.

She twiddled her fingers. Hoping for a word to slip his lips. What could she do that wouldn't make the line on his forehead bigger? Probably nothing. Even feeling his pain, she couldn't let him think Samuel was a fiend. Her friend had been nothing but kind to her. "Barrington?"

He leveled his shoulders. His gaze slowly drifted to hers. She'd seen him happy, flirtatious, and breaking-bricks-with-his-hands mad. This was so different.

She fingered a button on her coat. "The vicar's not the Dark Walk Abductor. You know that, Barrington."

He rubbed his chin. "No, I don't believe so. But, he's a part of this puzzle. It's time to put all the pieces together."

His gray eyes were tiny. He seemed so very different from the man who kissed her goodbye this morning.

With a tap to the ceiling, he brought the carriage to a halt. "Stay here. I need to get something."

She leaned close to the window and counted maple leaves.

A few minutes later, he returned. In his hands was a porcelain dish. He placed it onto her lap and curled a spoon into her fingers. "Eat, it will make you feel better. You'll be able to tolerate more food when your stomach is settled. I remember."

She opened the container and tunneled into the lemon verbena ice. The citrus smell teased her nose, almost forcing a smile. Last year, he'd been so pleased when she'd told him she carried his babe. He held her snug in an embrace. His full lips formed the widest grin.

Like today, he'd taken her to Gunter's. And her heart was so proud to have brought him joy. So proud. Her cheek felt wet. She swiped at it.

"Amora, eat. It will make you feel better."

She took a scoop and shoved it between her teeth. One dip upon her tongue should've made everything better, but it didn't. Barrington was too good of a man to be saddled with a wife like her, a possible vict...

No, she couldn't say that name. Her monster needed a true surname.

The carriage wound its way through London until it made it to Mayfair. She looked down. Half the bowl of ice had disappeared.

Very gently, Barrington lowered her to the ground and ushered her inside.

When Mrs. Gretling came for his hat and coat, he waved her away.

"Keep Mrs. Norton company."

Mrs. Gretling looked toward Barrington, curtsied and then disappeared.

Barrington led Amora into the parlor, then pivoted to the front door.

"Where are you going?"

He stopped and went to the window, peering out the glass. "Good, your mother and Wilson have arrived. I'll return by 10:30. The house will be lively. There will be no need to be concerned."

"We should talk. Last night, we were a team putting

the pieces together. Remember?"

He took off his spectacles and rubbed at his eyes. "We are not a team. I'm a man trying to hold onto a dream that's getting harder to see. I need to go meet with Hessing and Beakes. I have to figure out how much they suspect about Miller being in my custody."

"That sounds dangerous. Can't you beg off and stay with me?"

"Why, because the wife who doesn't love me, who sends me mistresses, wants me here? That's not a good reason." He leveled his top hat. His sharp tone softened. "Finish the ice. I'll return at 10:30. I won't have you fretting."

The door to the cellar creaked open. Footsteps pounded in the hall. Was Miller better?

A stocky black man with a deep chestnut complexion peered his head through the threshold. "Barrington, you've done it."

Her husband folded his arms. "Hudson, you were supposed to be gone by now. Mrs. Norton, you remember my cousin, Hudson Solemn."

The fellow shook his head. He then seemed to fix his gaze on Barrington as if Amora was invisible. "I have to leave a watcher with this one. The lad is a good one. And your guest is pretty bad off."

Barrington's face clouded. His shoulders seemed to droop as if more weights had been placed upon his back. "Thank you, Hudson. Let me drop you to your residence. It's on my way."

"Cousin, this is not the way to be ushered back to town, embroiled in your scandal." Hudson laughed, his green silk print waistcoat wrinkled with the effort. "I'm the black sheep, remember? Your man is definitely hooked on Dover pills. My young boy will give him some milky water as I call it to keep him calm for now."

Barrington looked so tired. He rubbed his neck. "You have a son?"

Hudson smiled a bit. "No, just repaying a debt. He's my charge."

Her husband raised his head to the door. He released a sigh that sounded strangled. "I'm not in a position to ask questions. Seems, I'm in those straits more and more. Thank you. Let me send you on your way."

Hudson bent and tugged at fine leather boots with a shiny engraved buckle. He obviously didn't know of the mourning rituals occurring in London. Amora had only met him once, many Yuletides ago, but he seemed much more affluent now. What had he done with himself in the passing years?

"You're welcome, Norton. I'm staying in the Rookery, drop me there."

Barrington shut the door just shy of a slam as they trudged outside. He should've slammed it, that would have made the broken pieces of Amora's spirit feel better.

As if sand shifted beneath her feet, she slunk to the sofa and put the cold bowl on her stomach. Madder than a hornet, Barrington sought danger before men who could imprison him or worse.

She'd pushed him to a place beyond anger, into recklessness. What harm could come to her husband if he were careless on the streets of London? She peered toward the cellar door as she stuffed a spoonful of melting ice into her mouth. Barrington placed himself in danger for Mr. Miller. Was the fellow worth it?

Something in her head said he was, but the shadows in

her mind couldn't be trusted. With the last possible Sarah in Bedlam, the girl's words wouldn't be either. How could Amora know if the man in the cellar was worthy of Barrington's sacrifices? Her gaze flicked to the cellar door again. There had to be a way to find out.

Chapter Five: A Dangerous Dinner

Barrington forced another cut of dry fowl down his throat. He needed to appear normal in the gaming atmosphere of Brooks's, his mentor's gentlemen's club, not piqued at Hessing's insipid lecture on dealing with mistresses.

But what was normal?

A Bedlamite in his basement, a pregnant wife who didn't love him. Well, didn't love him enough. Was this the meaning of being unequally yoked?

Hessing swirled his brandy. A few drops of the dark liquid drizzled down the tall sides of the crystal glass which he aptly lapped upon a finger and stuck into his greedy mouth. "Norton, you've been very quiet. I suppose an afternoon of reading my notes on the Dark Walk abduction cases dimmed your spirit or desire to aid a friend."

Barrington had read them all before in his quest to figure out if Smith, the man he'd sent to the gallows, had been telling the truth and then again when he saw how similar Amora's story was with the Dark Walk Abductor's victims. "Yes, they are very sad, very evil accounts."

Hessing's put down his drink and elbowed Beakes who sat to his left. "I remember this barrister's curiosity sitting at my table when he finished up at the university. I thought the war would dull his intellect, but it didn't. You came back hungrier, eager to prove yourself. Have you forgotten that fire, Norton?"

Barrington remembered those days too. He had admired Hessing's logical mind and work ethic. Yet, as those memories grew cold, he'd overlooked the man's growing avarice and womanizing. "I was very grateful for your tutelage. You know that. What is this Dark Walk business to you? You don't need another accolade."

The man laughed and swallowed another gulp of his brandy. "A knighthood might go to the man who delivers this villain. A knighthood is always desirable."

Barrington forced a rumble to match the men's laughter. A year ago, he might've seen the humor in the naked ambition. Blast it, he would compete for such a title as more proof of how well he'd done. Proof that others like him should be given a chance at education and opportunity. Now, he only cared about preserving what remained of his family and maybe saving a friend.

"See, Beakes? Norton just needed to think of the kill again. That feeling of winning."

With a snort, the solicitor folded his arms and leaned on the table, but then jerked up as if it dawned upon him not to put his elbows there. "Very fancy in here, Hessing."

Well, growing up poor restricted almost as much as being caught between races, Barrington thought to himself as he traced the molded laurel swags rimming the room.

"Norton, I've worked with ye a number of years. I wasn't excited at first, but your work ethic and winning streak won me over."

Sitting back in his chair to ensure his eyes didn't roll at the idle praise, Barrington glanced at the gentlemen filling the drawing room. He eyed their crisp cravats. Some still wore the traditions of powdered hair or a little longer like the Duke of Cheshire who'd just walked inside.

The crowds stilled.

The duke wasn't alone. Wilberforce and Macauley, the abolitionists he'd thrown his lot with, accompanied him.

Beakes sat back gritting his teeth. "There go the reformers heading to the Great Subscription Room. You think their egos will hit the vaulted ceiling?"

Barrington grimaced. "They're good men."

Hessing sipped at his Brandy. "Cheshire's becoming a leading advocate for ending slavery in all of England's colonies. I suppose you applaud such efforts, Norton?"

"Yes. I do." He said the words without hesitating or weighing out how his statement would be judged. "Right is right, gentlemen. And the law must be used to right wrongs. That's why it must be used to convict the true Dark Walk Abduct…"

Catching the duke's gaze, Barrington picked up his glass of water and started gulping. He'd made no progress on that gentleman's concerns. Nor was he likely to at this rate.

He balled a fist under the table. The urge to do more rattled in his truth-loving bones. Was it so wrong to forget the greater good and selfishly focus on his family?

The duke pivoted and headed to one of the more private rooms.

Hessing put his drink down then. "You know Cheshire, Norton?"

"I met him last year when he invited my wife and I to his grand ball, the one introducing his new duchess."

"An interesting new duchess." Beakes snickered and not in a good-enthralled-by-her-beauty way.

He chuckled again. "Not much is known of the duchess's family or upbringing, yet. Wonder if it is her influence making Cheshire so determined to fight these strange causes?"

Barrington almost spit the water he sipped back into his glass. He lowered it and glared at Beakes. "I have no doubt that you will find or invent gossip, but why bother a man fighting for principles? And, Hessing, you know I am very grateful for your tutelage. So let's get to the point of this."

Beakes tapped his curled fingers as if he held a cigar. With no smoking in this room of the club, the man must suffer a little. Good.

His solicitor leaned forward. "Here's some gossip I know is true. You dipped from the same trough. A wife and doxy from the same town is stupid, or arrogant. You're a rich man. You could procure a more discreet ladybird in London. I'm sure enough coins will make them forget your mixed blood."

"Like you, Beakes? You've made a good deal of coins working for this mixed blood."

The solicitor raised a brow. "Why would you risk all to help the singer? She must be a pretty fine piece."

Barrington leaned in. The need to strike something, to bury a fist into the blowhard's face pressed. It curled every knuckle tight as his care about what anyone thought dropped away. "Accuse me at your peril,

Beakes."

The man guffawed, then growled. "I know it was you who took the man claiming to be Miller from Bedlam. I'll find where you're hiding him. No one makes me look foolish before the magistrate, no matter how many coins I've earned."

Hessing put a hand on Beakes' shoulder. "Easy. Norton's not stupid enough to actually have taken the man, but I suspect he knows where the lunatic can be found. Convince Miller to turn himself over to the law, Norton. A bit of fluff or blackmail is not worth throwing away a career."

Yet, Barrington was stupid enough. Not thinking. Purely reacting, as he was now about to further ruin his good reputation with a fight at Brooks's. He relaxed his palms. "Why is a missing mental patient of your interests, Hessing? I understand Beakes. He doesn't like having his nose tweaked. But you, sir, what is this business for you?"

His mentor smirked and sat back in his velvet-tufted chair. "That knighthood. I want my last trial to be the greatest. I want to deliver the Dark Walk Abductor."

A few heads whipped at the pronouncement. Whispers again flew from one side of the room to the other. For a second time tonight, no gaming, no loud clapping for outlandish bets occurred. Just simple silence and accusatory stares.

Barrington shrugged it off and took another hack at his dinner. "That is a good thing to strive for."

Beakes grabbed his arm, stopping Barrington from taking another dehydrated bite. "Why help a deserter? I know a couple of runners who look forward to bringing him in. And when word gets out that you are in league with the villain, no one will help you."

The grandfather clock in the corner chimed.

Barrington shook free and pulled out his pocket watch. Ten o'clock. If he left now, he'd still be on time to Mayfair. For once, he was glad to keep Amora's schedule. Pushing to his feet, he dropped a coin in front of Beakes, then wiped his fingers on a napkin and tossed it down on the table as well. "Well, I'll make sure the next time I see Miss Miller or her brother, I'll tell them you want them to turn themselves in to the magistrate."

"You don't pay, Norton. The meals are part of my membership."

"My grandfather taught me to never owe anyone. Even things that are free cost you. Good evening, gentlemen."

Hessing nodded, though a frown plastered his face.

Barrington grabbed his hat from the entry and trudged out of the club. The low fog blocked the light of the stars.

A hard set of footfalls sounded from behind. He spun but saw nothing. He picked up his pace.

Rotating toward the mews, he trudged onward. When a shadow overtook him, Barrington realized his first mistake. He should've had James waiting for him directly.

The second was turning his back to the door of the club.

Before he could evade the blow, something heavy crashed into him. He tripped. Another blow to the base of his skull brought him to his knees. His glasses fell and shattered.

Barrington pivoted to strike back, but a piece of pipe struck his shoulder knocking him forward. His chest bounced hard against the sidewalk. All the air pushed from his lungs.

A faceless blob kicked his ribs. Pow. The blow landed soundly right into his hip. "For her!"

Spittle flopped onto Barrington's face. He couldn't move. He lay with his hands over his skull, trying to protect himself.

It was good he didn't kill the vicar today. Somebody needed to be with Amora to help raise his child in case Barrington couldn't. A knife blade stabbed him in his side, ushering in pure darkness.

Chapter Six: A Peek in the Cellar

Amora pulled the curtain back from the parlor window and stared outside. The fog shrouded her view of the street but there was nothing.

No carriage.

No horse team.

No Barrington.

She pattered down the hall to his study twice to check the clock on his mantle. It was well past 11:40. He'd never been out this late, not without sending a note. Where was he?

Her head sagged. She paced again to the parlor, posture slouching. Once more, she wrapped her hands in the curtains and rented them wide. Stillness. Hazy fog blocked most of the light. Nothing to light anyone's path.

How could he be so late? Barrington didn't break promises, even when he should. Her pulse raced, pounding harder and harder in the quiet town home. Something must've happened.

She slipped the sheers through her fingers, pushed away from the window curtain and wound deeper into her shawl. Why did her mind work this way? He could be delayed with a client or laboring hard at Lincoln's Inn, not thrown into Newgate. Not hurt.

He was fine. All was well with him. She started to pace again. Maybe she should paint. Images of trees, Vaux Hall's trees kept popping into her head. She sat down at the large canvas Samuel had retrieved from the attic, but couldn't bear to concentrate. She paced anew.

She walked at least two miles within the parlor. Her pulse remained even until the gong of Barrington's clock. Another cruel, fretful hour passed and no husband had arrived. Guilt overtook her heart, giving it a mighty squeeze. She'd pushed him away. She'd disappointed him again and again. How could she expect he'd want to come back to her?

But Barrington Norton was a man of his word. He didn't shift his thoughts like snow blowing in the wind. He was steady and loyal. She should never have treated him as if he had been an adulterer. She should never have pushed him to see how much his love would endure, never should have punished him because of her own failings.

She shook her head and adjusted her nightgown about her ankles. Not knowing what to do, she traipsed to the stairs and sank upon the lowest one. Sitting here, she wouldn't miss him if he came from the mews or the front entry.

Waiting for any noise, her thumb traced her belly in the same light manner Barrington did. His baby. She carried their baby!

The night she told Barrington of being abducted, he held her, made her feel so loved, so accepted. They made another miracle.

Her fingers trembled, vibrating the fringe of her creamy shawl. Would this baby survive to breathe air? Would she hold this one and feel his tiny heart beating against her bosom? Or would she shed those tears again as the doctor carried him away in soiled blankets?

A sob stuck in her throat. Another week and this child would just about have outlived the last. Too much can happen in seven days, starting with his father not coming home, never coming home.

Hyperventilating, she gripped her wrists. *Calm down.* For the baby, she needed to control her thoughts. Neither of them would survive if she didn't keep her panic at bay.

After a long breath, she eased her back against the steps. She patted her abdomen and recalled Barrington's angry face from this afternoon. The tightness of his countenance seemed as if the muscles of his jaw would pop.

But he was alive and well. That was the image she would keep in her head and her heart. "Your father's pretty mad at me."

She loosened her robe, slacking the sash. "What are we going to do?"

She distracted herself with counting. Thirteen boards between the edge of her toes and the dimmed wall sconces. It wasn't working. Where was he? What had stopped him from coming home to her?

A noise creaked from behind. Her heart froze. The cellar door pushed from its frame, exposing an opening. A low moan spilled out.

Her gaze whipped upstairs. Mama might awaken. Samuel or one of the children could hear. She popped up and pressed the door closed.

The vicar had stayed to chat with Barrington, hoping he'd return sooner. Then he discovered Mr. Miller. Samuel had looked almost as mad as Barrington, but someone had to check on Mr. Miller after supper.

What if Miller was in need of help? She looked again up the stairs. It was too late to get Samuel.

She stroked the door with her fingers tracing the grain. A quick look couldn't hurt anything. Before her mind lost courage, she started into the cellar. Her bare feet slapped against the creaking treads as she descended.

Samuel had left the sconces burning, so Amora's fears were abated at least for now. Her breathing leveled, her pulse calmed. She could do this.

A moan...no, a man's tortured cry reached her ear. "Norton? Cynthia?"

Though Amora could understand the words, the mournful tone sounded like a wounded animal. Was Gerald Miller in pain? Was he crazed?

She paused mid-step, then straightened her shoulders. She didn't have the luxury of throwing stones, not when she needed answers. Why had she heard Mr. Miller's voice in her captor's cell?

The answer would prove if the man was worthy of whatever trouble Barrington was in. She had to know.

"Augh. Help." The moan sounded so harsh, so lonely.

Amora planted her feet onto the cellar floor.

A young boy slept outside the door. He was dark with freckles on his nose and a tangle of curly short cropped hair.

She took off her shawl and wrapped it about him like a blanket. It wasn't chilly down here. Nevertheless, it should bring the boy comfort.

A smile lifted her lips when he tucked himself into

fabric. His small snore lifted the fringe.

Miller moaned again. Then said, "Nort...on."

She stood up, listening to the cries. Should a doctor be called?

Sweat beaded on her brow. She'd call one of the leeching class, those evil doctors, if it meant helping someone in pain.

The groaning became louder. "Nor...ton!"

If she knew where her husband was, she'd tell. And if he were here, Barrington would be in the cellar, caring for his friend, insisting Amora return to her chambers like an obedient, fragile girl.

She lifted her head and took another step toward the door. Even a delicate vase when broken had sharp shards. "It will be fine. This man won't hurt me."

Even if Mr. Miller was in league with her abductor, he didn't sound as if he could cause any more harm.

Capturing a breath, she pushed on the door.

As the opening grew bigger, the light of the room illuminated Mr. Miller, emaciated and frail, lying on a mattress. With legs as thin as a fallen branch, he stared ahead. His feet, so small and shriveled, kicked against the blanket. This picture seemed so different from the thin but healthy man who lived in Barrington's shadow.

Gerald turned his head toward her. He licked his dry lips. "Help...me."

Heart beating fast, Amora entered and stepped closer. "You're safe here. You have to calm."

With a limb seemingly out of control, waving from side to side, he grabbed her palm. His hands were leathered and chapped. "Thirsty."

She broke free. His fingers dropped to the bed. With a quick pivot, she was at the door, but her tongue felt heavy.

Salty and dry. The same way her mouth became after feeding upon the scraps her abductor left. She'd hoped the monster would return to his senses and free her and the others, or at least given them water. How odd to hope for the devil to come and to hope he repent or die, all at the same time.

Thirst had dried her tongue then, so much so she couldn't cry anymore. And Amora had a lot of unshed tears. The monster had taken Sarah. She'd consented to his torture, so that he'd free her.

The screaming, the howling memories in her mind, shook her arms. Amora lifted vibrating fingers to her temples to block out the remembered pain. A voice, mid-range and clear in tone sounded. It was Miller's voice.

She opened her eyes and looked at the lump on the bed, but she saw him younger, as Barrington's friend, as a man who'd discovered where the abductor kept his victims.

"You tried to save me and Nan Druby. You're no monster."

With one look between his long auburn lashes into Mr. Miller's wet eyes, she saw the freshness of his confusion.

"Druby." His tone sounded so mournful.

Her heart broke for him. He was another victim, too. She put a shaky hand to her mouth. "You tried to save us, but something went wrong. Some water, I'll get you some water."

She rushed to the bed table and poured milky medicine smelling liquid from a clay pitcher. Stretching on tippy-toes, she held the mug to his mouth.

The liquid spilled down his cheek as he gulped. A few beads of it dribbled onto his muslin nightshirt. "Norton?"

"He's not here. You'll see him in the morning." He'd be back by then, right?

Miller nodded. The pillow swallowed his skull, cradling the flattened part behind his ear. Her heart clenched. What else could she do to help?

Whether it was her heart or lips that started singing first, she couldn't tell. But, she started to hum Barrington's song. "Amazing grace how sweet the sound."

Miller closed his eyes. His lips twitched as if he repeated the word, *sweet*, then he settled.

She wanted to press him for the location of her cell, but sat on her hands slowly singing the refrain.

Miller knew where he'd found Nan Druby and her. And his testimony must be enough to convince Barrington that neither he, nor her abductor was the Dark Walk monster.

She folded her hands, pulled her feet onto the low rung of the stool and continued to hum. Barrington would return soon. He'd get the answers. He just had too.

Chapter Seven: What Will He Do For Her

For her.

Barrington struggled to move. He had to get to her. Amora. It couldn't be too late. He'd promised her. Oh, God let her be well and not in a panic.

Something cold and wet hit his eyes. He tried to grab it but as he lifted his arm a burning sensation took hold of his chest. When the rag flopped again on his brow, he focused his energy on the thin flailing wrist mopping his face and caught it. "Amora, you're alright. Please be—"

"Sir, I am not Amora. Please unhand me."

"Yes, Norton." The heavier, autocratic voice sounded familiar. "I need you to unhand my wife."

Barrington released the soft palm and tried to sit up but couldn't. "My glasses please."

"They're broken, sir," the soft voice said.

When the blur handed him the broken lenses, he slipped them on moving them to see through the cracks. His pride stung as much as his ribs. A musket hung atop a roaring fireplace. He wasn't at Mayfair, unless his mother-in-law with her Egyptian magic had transformed it into a stately room three times as large and had tossed in a wall of books for good measure. "What?"

The duke of Cheshire and his wife hovered over him. "You're alright, Norton."

The duchess tugged on her long sleeves and draped a frilly shawl over her thin limbs. "Mr. Norton, do you feel well enough for tea?"

Tea? There was no time for tea. There was a thief out there who'd nearly killed him, and a wife at home who must be frantic. "No, Duke. Duchess. I mean, no tea."

He tried to sit up from the sleek upholstered chaise. A whimper almost escaped from his mouth. He buttoned his lips, catching it. Barrington lay back tugging at his opened shirt. His fingers caught on the bandages wrapping his side. "I'm sorry, your grace. Duchess."

"Cousin, you might want to stay flat for a while. You bled a bit, but nothing vital was permanently harmed. The duke had the good sense to leave the blade in you 'til I could fix you up."

Barrington rocked his head to squint. Hudson leaned against the bookcase. At this, he closed his eyes again. "I'll just wait for the nightmare to pass."

"It's not a nightmare," the duke said. "You are quite lucky. I saw you leaving. I went out the back of Brooks's to ask you of your progress on my project, only to frighten off a footpad attacking you."

"Project? A mere pickpocket? No. An attempted murderer, and he cut you too, dearest."

The duke stuffed his bandaged hand into his coat. "It's nothing."

The duchess put a hand on her hip. "When is it something? When the threats to hurt you grow even more? You're taking too many risks."

She walked over to him and put a hand to his cheek. "William, what will Mary and I do without you?"

The anguish and love in the lady's voice was thick.

The duke looked down, but grasped her palm within his. What could any husband say when their wives were right?

Hadn't Amora always been frightened of Barrington staying out late? Didn't she believe this would happen, that someone would gut him in the streets?

Barrington coughed and decided to help the man who'd saved him. "It was a thief, Duchess. Not someone upset over my or the duke's politics. He frightened him away. Thank you, Cheshire."

The duke didn't appear to be listening. His gaze was locked upon the woman clutching at his lapels, filling his embrace as if no one else was in the room.

Barrington looked away. He rifled over his person, palming his bruised rib. His money purse and Amora's present was still intact on his person. Duke truly must've frightened the thief away, unless it was no thief. What did he look like?

Before Barrington could mouth any questions or objections, a heavy knock sounded.

The duke smoothed his hair with his good hand, but there was blood on his jacket. "That must be someone from the magistrates."

"Oh, Lord Justice will be very upset at this hour. I'd rather not face him."

Cheshire nodded and went to the door. "I'll see what I can do."

When he left, the duchess started pacing. "He's doing too much, trying to right a wrong that is not his."

Barrington managed to sit this time. He tugged at his

soiled jacket, attempting to look as dignified as he could. "That's what a man does when he is in love."

The floorboards knocked with his cousin's firm steps. He came closer. "Yes, fools and love. You think you can stand?"

His head swam too much to attempt it without falling flat. "In a moment. Ma'am, would it be too much trouble for some of that tea?"

She almost smiled as if needing an excuse to go see about her husband. "I'll return shortly."

As soon as the door closed behind her, Hudson pounced. He leapt within a foot of the chaise. "So who is trying kill you? Was it over a white woman? I told you about messing with those light women."

Barrington pulled his feet to the floor. "I'll ignore your foolish talk since it's obvious you patched me up. How bad is it and how are you here?"

"You'll live." He flopped into a close chair. "Apparently you mumbled to the Duke and your man James to go get me. What a shock it was to find my paragon of a cousin steeped in trouble. So, who's having an affair? Not the little missus? I saw how angry you were when you dropped her to Mayfair?"

"If I didn't owe you, I'd probably call you out. My vows our intact." Barrington took a breath and shifted as the world's greatest headache raged within his skull. "Married people can argue. They should be able to do so without censure, or friends and family trying to wedge them apart. They should always be able to forgive."

Hudson reared back and laughed. "Who are you trying to convince? The bachelor in the room?"

Yes, who was Barrington trying to sway? Amora may not love him, but she would love their child. He just needed to stay alive long enough to make sure she and the baby would be well. Did anything else matter?

Chuckling, as if he knew he'd hit the right cord, Hudson sank deeper into the cushions. "I should've known something was amiss when James didn't return my little watch guard on time." He brushed the lapel of his dark coat. "You'd just come from Brooks's. Maybe someone didn't like coffee entering the front door of their creamy establishment. The help enters from the rear."

"Hudson, I don't know."

"Can it be a coincidence that you're rescued by one of the leading reformers trying to end slavery in England's colonies?"

Someone had tried to kill Barrington. The danger started to thaw in his head. Being so focused on Beakes and Hessing, what signs of evil had he missed? He shook his pounding brainbox trying to remember the face of the assassin.

"Well, whoever it was, thief, angry husband, or anti-reformer, they hit a rib when they struck. You're lucky. They were aiming for your heart." Hudson lowered his voice. "Stop whatever it is you're involved with and remain my favorite living cousin. I've no interest in a dead one."

"Neither do I, Hudson."

The door opened and the duchess returned with a tray of tea and biscuits. "Mr. Solemn, please have something to refresh yourself. You worked very hard stitching up Mr. Norton and attending my husband."

Hudson glanced in the direction of the duchess. "No, ma'am. And the duke and the barrister are old military men. They're used to field surgery."

"Mr. Norton, are you able to take some warm tea?"

Barrington lifted a tired palm to wave her off, but the duchess didn't seem to pay attention. Her gaze drifted from him to Hudson's direction. With a nod, he lifted his chin to the offered cup. "Ask your question. My cousin just finished with his."

She bit her lip and then adjusted her spectacles. "What is it like?"

Barrington balanced the cup within his shaking hands. "What is what like?"

She adjusted her spectacles. "To know who and what you are, from the beginning."

Hudson's forehead scrunched up. Though Hudson's own sister could pass for white, perhaps he hadn't seen a mulatto with such a high rank. Or one so open about it. "Does the reforming duke know? Or is this why he's so consumed?" He asked.

"My husband knows. Love conquered all, the differences and even the earnest misunderstandings. But, you two haven't answered my question. I didn't know that I was a black. I grew up being treated differently by my family and didn't know why."

Hudson pursed his lips and shook his head. "You clean up well."

Barrington groaned and set down the tea. "What my cousin should say, if he had any bit of sense, is that you are who you are. And you live each day in expectation of what more you can do."

Hudson stood. His head shook so much, Barrington thought it might fall off, roll along the floor and out the door. He crossed his arms over his silvery-gray waistcoat. "Tell her of the suspicions and constant reminders of not belonging. The threats for trying to live and do."

"I won't. I've made my way and so have you, cousin. We've both taken the opportunities that have been afforded and created ones that didn't exist."

"Even stolen them when necessary." Hudson's voice held both mocking notes and leftover hurt from their youth.

"So the duke knows and doesn't care." Hudson chuckled. "The great snowy-white liberator."

The duchess lifted her head. Poise radiated her pretty face. "Yes, my husband knows. And no, he doesn't care. I cared more. He saw me when no else did and he's given me love that overflows my heart. But he knows of the prejudice we may face so he's trying to make this world better for me and if he can't, he'll take the family abroad. He's willing to change his whole life. He loves me that much. And I love him enough to keep him from doing so."

Swaying, Barrington stood. Sheer will kept him from pitching over. He let the pain rush through him, ravaging its way all the way down his spine. He had to get back to Amora. That was all that mattered. But, could he do as the duke and change everything about his life to make Amora happy and secure? "Love is an opportunity, Duchess. One more need to take. Tell the duke, I am grateful. I'm in his debts."

"Well, I salute your opportunity, Norton, nearly being killed in an alley. Good evening, Duchess. We'll find our opportunity through the kitchen where all the other mulattos like me and pure blacks are expected to use. Norton, your man James awaits with your carriage out back in the mews."

Hudson stormed across the room and grabbed Barrington's arm. His anger at life hadn't dimmed.

However, Barrington couldn't help him, just Amora. "Come on, Barrister."

How much was Barrington willing to give up to keep Amora well? And could he do so without the great love that Cheshire and his duchess shared?

Barrington leaned more of his weight onto his stocky cousin. "Thank the duke for me. I must get home to my wife."

Chapter Eight: Pharaoh-In-Training

Amora eased off the stool as a low snore left Mr. Miller.

The poor man looked so frail. His shaking had slowed the deeper he fell into sleep.

A hundred bitter questions were on her tongue. Where was she held? Why was Mr. Miller there? Did he see the monster?

The sourness was so thick. She fought against shaking his arm to awaken him. It wasn't good to disturb his rest, even for the truth. For the first time, she understood Barrington's battles. He loved truth, but he also cared for others.

She sighed and drew her arms about her. Perhaps tomorrow Mr. Miller would be better. It was only a few more hours till dawn. Surely her own nightmares could stay away too. Maybe she'd go upstairs and paint. The easel and canvas that Samuel had brought down called to her from the parlor.

Did she truly need to know tonight where the monster kept her? How could she bear it with no Barrington to hold her and keep her safe?

A chill wrapped about her limbs, shaking her newly stirred resolve. The formless monster of her memories didn't need a face tonight.

She slipped to the door and eased from the room. She took a final look, allowing her fingers to rest on the cold brass doorknob. Her soul was in knots. Where was Barrington?

With a shake of her head, she cleared her eyes of thieves and carriage accidents, all the logical things that could've harmed him. Then there were the irrational ones, like the monster finally killing him as he promised all those years ago.

That was silly. Crazy to consider.

Her eyes adjusted to the darkness shrouding her.

She gazed toward the top of the stairs. The sconces were out. Had they died whilst she visited Miller or had they been snuffed?

Peering down, she noticed the boy had disappeared. Perhaps he snuffed them before leaving.

Fear made her toes cold. She shifted her feet as she rubbed her temples. The boy was real. The sconces had been lit or she would never had come down the stairs. This was real.

She cracked Miller's door open wider to add more light to her path, but it was still dark. If she waved her arms she could find the bottom rail and count treads until she made it to the top. She wasn't going to panic. She could do this without slipping headlong into fear.

The child inside her needed her to be calm.

Humming Barrington's song of grace once more, she moved a little. Her arms flailed searching for the staircase.

Before she could take two full steps, a shadow moved at the bottom of the stairs. It charged toward her, covered her mouth and captured her in arms of iron.

The stench of sweat and possibly blood surrounded her. She screamed into the muffling hand.

She punched and kicked and fought. No one was going to take her, not ever again. Power surged within her limbs. She kicked at the man's thick legs and hit at his chest until he whimpered and slid to the floor. The crack of light spilling from Miller's room exposed tawny brown skin and wide gray eyes.

"Barrington?"

It was him, writhing in pain on the floor. Heart in her throat, she fell upon him, pulling him into her arms as much as she could. "Be all right."

It took more than a moment for him to say anything. Instead, a shaking palm touched her cheek. He simply stared at her.

With a low groan, he cleared his throat. "I should know better than to sneak up on you."

She fell on him again. She hugged him tightly. It sounded as if he couldn't breathe. Maybe he couldn't. She arose and looked at him.

There were bruises on the side of his face. Even in the dim light, she could see his shirt had stains. "What happened to you? Why are you so late? Don't you know I frighten thinking someone has taken you from me?"

He tugged her chin, smoothed his fingers over her lips and across her cheek as if trying to smooth away the fear surely etched upon her countenance. "I'm here now."

There wasn't just heat in his eyes. Something richer made the gray pools turn into molten silver. She looked back to his cut open shirt. "Where were you?"

"I was set upon by a footpad. I'm fine. But…"

"But what?"

"May I just hold you? One more time. I almost didn't come home."

His admission echoed in her ear. It penetrated her chest deeply and rattled around the void she allowed to live inside. She didn't want to be empty. She didn't want to lose Barrington.

She sank into his arms, resting against him.

His tucked about her. A whisper left him that sounded like, "I'm home."

It was half-dark. Barrington smelled horrid. And yet, she'd never felt safer. He was alive. No one took him away.

Not enough time passed before he moved. He shifted her to his side and sat up with a loud groan.

"Amora?" His tone toughened becoming accusatory. "What are you doing down here? I thought I was catching an evildoer."

She popped up and sat alongside him. "Mr. Miller started crying. He called for you. I had to help him before he woke the whole house. It's not just Mama here. The vicar and his children stayed. He saw that I was very distraught when you left."

"You should've sent Wilson down here and taken no risks. You promised me."

"You promised to be home on time. I sent the vicar earlier, when you didn't come home at 10:30."

Barrington huffed, a combination sounding of disapproval and pain. "What did he think of our guest?"

She played with a button on her husband's waistcoat remembering Samuel questioning Barrington's competence. "He's quite upset."

A heavy breath steamed from Barrington's lips. "I'm upset with myself, too. I'm bringing not only scandal to us, but danger. What am I going to do?"

She folded her arms. She wouldn't argue with him, not with him half-lying on the floor. She glimpsed the top of the stairs. "Let's get you up. Do I need to find James?"

"No. He's dropping my cousin and his charge to their lodgings." Barrington tried to garner the power to stand, but his hip didn't seem to want to obey.

He must be hurting. It was so like him to not say so.

She offered him a hand.

He stared at her for at least a minute before he grasped her fingers. Slowly at first, then with more energy, he rose using her strength as leverage. Wincing in the dim light, he laid his back against the wall. "How is Miller?"

"He quieted with a drink of the milky water. Being thirsty is terrible. It can make everything hurt. Your tongue burns."

"Like with the pig scraps your abductor fed you." Barrington's head dipped, his words spilled out. "I don't care how thirsty Miller is. He could've hurt you."

She put a palm to his chest. Her pinky sliding into bandaging. He was hurt badly. "Barr, what happened?"

"Help me out of here. I want you away from him."

She wanted to protest, to prove to him she'd figured more things out by coming down here. But there was no room in his command for discussion. She nodded, acquiescing to the fact that he'd never see her side of things.

He draped his arm atop her shoulder. She helped him to the stairs. Slowly and carefully, they made it tread by tread.

Maybe she was a help to him. Maybe not, giving her short height to his. But the higher they got, the slower he became and the more she could feel his weight bearing down upon her.

That's when it struck her. Though he wouldn't voice it, he did need her. "You call Mama stubborn."

"Must be rubbing off living with both of you."

Tiring herself, they reached the main floor of Mayfair. He lumbered past her as she closed the cellar door.

She turned toward him and gasped.

The bright light of the hall exposed the beating he'd taken. Blood matted his jacket and his shirt. The bruising on the side of his head made her heart tremble. Her deepest fears were coming true.

He pulled at his coat as if self-conscious. A box fell from his pocket.

He winced as he tried to pick it up. She grabbed it for him. "What is this? Why would a thief leave jewelry behind?"

A grimace filled his silent face.

"Why are you carrying jewels? Where were you?" She opened it and exposed bits of folded paper. There were notes twisted like the ones she used to remind herself of things. "I don't understand."

"On the balcony at Hessing's party, I saw the messages spill from your reticule. I thought I'd pen you a few to encourage you."

She unfolded one. *More than a conqueror.* Another said, *Trust your heart.* Another, *Trust Barrington.* Her eyes dampened.

"Say something, Amora. I know things are wrong between us. If it's too personal or if it makes you sad, you don't have to keep it."

"It's the best gift." Part of her wanted to leap into his arms and kiss him, but right now he looked as if he'd fall over.

Clutching his gift to her bosom, she licked her lips and looked away from the searching look in his eyes. "Are you going to tell me what happened? Or do you not trust me enough to handle the truth?"

He shook his head then clasped the wall as if he needed to steady himself. "I trust you, Amora. Just like those bits of paper say. But, this is bigger than that. Someone tried to kill me."

"I knew it. Like I always knew it. He said he would."

"Amora, who said they'd kill me?"

She put a hand to her mouth. That awful taste of fear had returned to her tongue. She withdrew her fingers to her side and squared her shoulders. "The monster. As he taunted Sarah about her father dying, he taunted me about killing you."

"He knew my name. He knew Sarah's father. The devil knew his victims."

Barrington turned from her, muttering things she couldn't quite make out. He hobbled over and sank upon the stairs. "That's why you fear my being out late. It wasn't to control me or being in want of attention. It was him. Again, he's lodged between us."

He put his hands to his face and righted his broken spectacles. "No more. He's taking no more. You hear me, Amora? No more."

She came to him, kneeling at his side. "I don't want him to have anything else either."

Grunting, he drew her up to his side, so that she shared the step. "Lying on the street, thinking about dying helped me make up my mind about our marriage."

"By yourself?" She wanted to tug away, but not when she'd almost lost him. Hearing his heart pounding in her ear was too sweet. "And what have you decided?"

"Those blasted papers your mother is peddling will be burned. I won't give up my rights and let my child go. My career's falling apart, everyone at the Lincoln Inn thinks I'm an adulterer, and *you* can't wait to leave London. I won't lose another thing, not one more thing."

His low tone vibrated like when he grieved his grandfather. She knew Barrington's lecturing voice. This wasn't it. "Listen to me." He reached for her hand and slipped their linked palms to her abdomen. "You're carrying my child. My son or daughter will not know a month, a week, if I can help it, a day without hearing my voice. I want to be the rock upon which they anchor themselves, like Grandfather and good old Mr. Tomàs. You won't…you can't deprive me of that. As close as you were to your own father, you know what it means to a child. You know what it means to have a father's love."

The word *sorry* rose in her throat. Even if she clenched her teeth, she couldn't stop the hated word from leeching out. "Sorry. I'm so sorry for inciting Cynthia."

He slipped a little more on the step. "I still think my gifts are more thoughtful than yours."

Barrington, trying to be humorous, had just told her she couldn't leave London. "But Tomàs Manor is so much better than here to wean a baby."

He craned his neck to the ceiling. "I have rights as to where my family will be."

She'd feared him putting her away, but she'd never thought he'd use his authority to separate her from their baby. Her breath came in pants. "You would take… this child from me?"

A hundred different emotions washed over his cheeks. He put his hands on her shoulders as if he'd shake her, but he drew her against him again. "Never. I wouldn't hurt you or our baby, but I'm not going to be led in this spiral chase anymore. You don't know what you want, and you keep forgetting who I am."

He released her and leaned back as if the next tread would right his spine. "Our marriage will remain intact, if only in name. But, we can work together to rear this miracle. You and this child will be with me. We can do this together for our family's sake."

"What happens if I can't bring this one to be birthed?"

He ripped at his coat. "You will be well because I now understand. I'll do everything to put you at ease and make sure you're healthy and secure."

Her brow furrowed. She was just another burden upon his broad shoulders. "You didn't think about involving me in this decision? I don't have a say?"

"Frankly, you've told me all I need to know. I had to decide how much I am willing to change." He teetered and slouched further. His motion was awkward and stiff. "I needed to be comfortable in the notion that if I must abandon London, even practicing law, I could do so and have no regrets."

Abandon London? Leave the law? So many times she'd wanted that, but it wouldn't solve anything. He'd resent her more. "You love practicing law in London."

"I love you...your dream of a family. I'll do what I must, including turning in my best friend."

"But, he's not guilty. You'd be sentencing him to death. And I remember. He came to save Nan Druby and myself."

He squinted at her, then shrugged his shoulders. "I

can't talk of this anymore." He launched up and swayed. "I'm going to go to bed."

She slipped his arm over her shoulder again and guided him to the next step. "You can't. Your bed is occupied."

His thin smile disappeared. "Wilson couldn't wait to take my place."

"No." Concentrating, she aimed his foot to the successive tread. "The Wilson children are sleeping in your chambers. It was the closest to mine and to these stairs."

"Where's their father?"

"In the last guest room. It was far too late to send them away. Once he knew of Miller, he wasn't going to leave women in the house alone, unprotected. With Mama in the other guest room, all the beds upstairs are full."

He sucked in a breath and climbed the rest of the stairs. "Then I'll sleep in the master's bed chamber." He patted her arm and led her to the rooms.

She reached for his shoulder. "But the children."

Sliding out of his tattered coat, he undid the buttons to his vest as if he'd strip right in the open. "I'm talking of your room, maybe I should say Pharaoh-in-training's room. I'm going to sleep in that wide bed of yours."

She'd pushed him to the edge. He'd lost his reason. The candlelight of the sconce reflected on his chest, a tuft of curly hair peeking from his opened shirt.

"You do need to rest, and Mr. Miller is expecting to see you in the morning."

"My friend's truth can wait. I wish to stretch out on a mattress so I can walk without a limp when the sun rises." He held out his hand to her. "You need to rest, too. That is the most important thing."

She studied his hunched posture. His hip must be aching.

"Hesitant? We are partners in this thing. I'm sure we can sleep platonically. You can stay to your side, right? And if you are destined to be barefoot and pregnant, keep those cold toes off me."

A soft chuckle left her mouth. If a foolhardy notion was the price to keep his anger at bay or even offer the remote chance she'd not awaken alone, it had to be acceptable. "But you will stay through the night in my bed? Not get up to work?"

"I am tired enough to be immobile for several days. Hopefully, you don't mind."

The problem was she didn't mind, not one whit.

Barrington studied the lift in her brow, the sparkle in her eye. She wasn't saying *no*. The notion was bacon-brained. An invention of the moment, an off-color joke created after discovering she'd given away his bed.

He yawned and let tired air eke from his lungs, probably the only thing keeping him upright at this point. Leaning against her door, he lifted his head. "Well, Pharaoh II, do you get to have a roommate? I don't think I can make it down to my study."

She licked her lips and raised a hand to him. "Yes."

He clasped her palm and stared into her violet eyes. He had had a completely horrible day and now she stood looking at him agreeing to foolishness.

His defenses melted a little.

Her chilled fingers warmed within his palm. If there had been no vicar and no clod-headed response to her admission of being abducted, would Barrington still possess all of her heart?

She opened her door and led him to a chair by her vanity.

A laugh or maybe a yell welled inside, itching his skin. His intention to go upstairs to retrieve a nightshirt now turned into an opportunity to stretch his limbs against a firm mattress, near a soft wife. Maybe he needed to be ridiculous all the time around her in order to regain her love.

"You'll need something to wear." She picked at her sleeve as her gaze tangled with his. Her tidy chignon had shed a few raven locks that curled near her eyes.

He plucked at his musty shirt. This was a bad idea. With her sensitivity to smells, he must be a wonderful bouquet of pavement and perspiration. Worse, blood. "I think—"

"Sit." She put the jewelry box on her bedside table and lit a small candle. "I'll be right back." She eased from the room.

Struggling not to wake the house with his whimpers, he pulled off one boot then the other. He dropped the sweaty leather with a gentle plop, placed his elbows on the glass surface and massaged his forehead. He looked horrid, felt dreadful. Someone had tried to kill him. There was no doubt about it.

How would she have fared when they told her? Would she be as strong as she was tonight or would the anxiety have hurt their child? She always feared something would happen to him. His shriveled heart lurched lower into his gut.

When she'd opened the jewelry box, he saw her heart shining in her eyes. She didn't hate him, but there was fear lighting her countenance. She was afraid to love him, to be vulnerable with him again. How would he ever regain her trust?

The door opened. Amora returned with his nightshirt hung about her neck like a shawl. In her arms, she juggled a candle and a bowl.

She looked absolutely beautiful with her brow furrowed in concentration. More raven tresses spilled from her chignon. "Little Jack's sleeping in the crib. We fetched it from the attic."

She'd been up in the attic again. So much for James' hiding tactics. Maybe Barrington should have something done about the space. That sounded like a project for his mother-in-law.

"Jackson looks like an angel." There were tears in her voice.

He had to keep her from sadness or this next child wouldn't sleep in it. Swallowing to extinguish his own angst, Barrington powered to stand a little too quickly and staggered. "I'll go clean up."

"No, you will let me take care of you. You only do so when you're anxious, like before a trial. Sit and accept my help. The Pharaoh-in-training has spoken."

Her tone sounded stern and her gaze locked upon his.

Maybe giving her purpose instilled determination. With more confidence, she might trust her heart and love him again. He dropped back into the chair and muffled another whimper. "Yes, ma'am."

Setting the candle on the floor, she took a pitcher from the vanity and poured it into her pan. A small tan bar floated atop the water. Her fingers settled on his shins. She wrenched off his stockings.

"You don't have to--"

"Quiet, Barrington. You'll wake up the children."

He closed his eyes as the soft damp cloth wiped against his skin. The coolness of the water, the gentle massaging of her thumbs against his heel... A sigh of contentment left his mouth. Joy in the midst of a storm.

The sound of water dripping from her wrung cloth filled his ear. She anointed his face and neck with bergamot.

He opened his eyes to witness her hovering over him, tending to the bruise on his skull. Such a beautiful face. She was always so generous when he let her fuss over him. She poured more water onto a cloth, giving it a good soaking then wiped into his hair.

There was something in Ephesians he'd read about washing her with the word, not vice versa, but Barrington didn't mind. She needed to feel of use to him, and he needed her.

It wasn't clear if she took off his shirt or if he helped. It didn't matter, not with the circular strokes of the cotton rag along his rib cage tracing the makeshift bandage.

"He hurt you badly." She brushed a tear from her cheek, then kept working. "What's under the dressing? Nastier bruises?"

"Let's not think of it. I'm all patched up because of my cousin."

She looked away, staring at his feet. A small sob mixed with another quivering breath. "I always knew he'd... you'd get hurt."

"I'm fine, Amora. You needn't cry."

With a nod, she kept working, refreshing the tight muscles of his back.

Regardless of how unsettled things were between them, there had to be some love inside her for him and when it mattered she wasn't too fearful to show it. That had to be love.

Maybe it could grow with their baby.

He slid a hand under her chin and lifted it. Gazing deeply into her eyes, he sought to slip through the walls shrouding her heart. "I'm here, Amora. I'm alive. I haven't left us."

She nodded, then handed him the washcloth and nightshirt. "You're almost ready to be my roommate. Hurry up, then dress."

She disappeared behind the gauzy curtain framing the canopy of the bed. Nothing could be better than the soft lawn fabric or her firm mattress.

Grunting, he changed into his long sleep garment and stashed his dusty clothes in a neat pile on the chair. He took his time with slow careful steps and moved to her bed. He climbed upon her mattress.

Eyeing him, Amora fluffed her pillow, then settled down upon it. "You know I sleep with a candle burning. No snuffing it."

"Yes, ma'am." He tugged at their shared blanket, marveling at how wide her eyes seemed in the dim light, how the small hint of smile upon her lips made her so lovely.

"Oh, I make no promises about where my toes end up. You're usually quite warm. Thanks for my present."

"You're welcome, and I'll be here when you awaken. I think that was the final term of the negotiation."

That former hint of a smile now covered her whole face. She snuggled into the bed sheets, rolling onto her side.

Her mindset, her composure possessed confidence. It had to be due to his allowing her to help. Giving her the sense he trusted her seemed to mean more than his affection.

Yet, he knew in his hurting gut she'd never be the carefree girl he proposed to so long ago. There was too much hurt in her to ever let his love enter without suspicion. Could he be content like this, not knowing if she'd awaken remembering his love or his folly? Maybe.

When she inched a little closer, he had half a mind to reach out and stroke her hair or to pull her into his arms, but that wasn't part of their bargain. Her heart was still very closed to his love. The vicar or the gulf of problems strangling their marriage held it at bay.

He stretched and shut his lids. Gerald Miller, Hessing, Beakes, the mystery, the man who tried to kill him; he'd figure out what to do with all of them tomorrow. For now, he'd revel in the feel of Amora's toes nestled along his shin and pretend it was a small piece of her soul reaching out to his.

Chapter Nine: Images of the Mind

The old canvasses and paints retrieved from the attic were just what Amora needed to stop fretting over Barrington. For a week, he claimed to be fine, but let her feed him and make him hot tea, even fuss about his pillows. That should've been a sign at how hurt his attacker left him.

Today, she'd caught sight of the wound under the wrappings when Mr. Solemn visited. She might be otherworldly, but she wasn't stupid. Barrington had been stabbed close to his heart. He could've died.

Forcing the dark images of every threat, every curse of her monster back into the shadows of her mind, she stood behind her easel and feathered in more streaks of amber. The painting had to have enough light. She needed to focus on it, not the darkness of what had happened or what could've happened.

With a final stroke, she achieved enough sun filtering between the limbs of the grove of trees she'd formed. Only having been to Vaux Hall once, it was difficult to be sure she'd captured the park just right, but the colors and forms felt true.

She stippled more red for the setting sun, as she listened to the light chuckles coming from the dining room and the occasional fall of a woman's slippers. But, no heavy heels pounded down the stairs. When she heard that deep noise, that would mean Barrington had recovered his strength. Deep in her soul, she knew he needed to be fully well. The truth of the past was coming, and everyone would need to be filled with strength to face it.

Her insides twisted with an extra portion of guilt. She loved fussing over Barrington. She liked waking up seeing him there. That was something he rarely did, for he always arose early to review trial notes.

Slippers clicked on the floorboards.

A light tick, tick produced her mother at the threshold. "Painting again? May I see?"

Quicker than she should, Amora shook her head. It wasn't perfect yet, and she wasn't sure she could weather her mother's criticism. "Not until it is done."

A pout swallowed Mama's lips. She tugged on her rich tanned gloves and started rolling an egret feather bonnet that matched her deep chocolate carriage dress. "Well, you seem more relaxed. All must be well in the Norton household. Have you two come to terms?"

Amora dipped her brush into her cup of water and stepped away from the canvas. What could she say? What words could hide the turmoil twisting inside her? She lifted her gaze again and offered the truth. "He said no separation."

Mama eyes widened as she nodded. "Seems right with a baby to come, but you…you don't want a family with your husband?"

With a shrug, she let the questions fade and turned to the window. She hooked her fingers within the lace loop of the new curtain's fringe. Mama had installed them yesterday.

"Amora, you didn't answer."

She couldn't share her thoughts with her mother or her husband. No answers lingered inside. It wasn't easy to cling to the warmth that stirred within her middle, not when she kept seeing a picture of Barrington looking over an empty crib. "What do you have planned today?"

"Stop it, Amora. You don't have to look for sadness. Look at the bowls of ice your husband has James bring you everyday. That treat alone should bring you joy. He's done this everyday since Vaux Hall, a week."

Pivoting toward her mother's voice, she tried to lift a smile, for the half eaten bowl of lemon ice was a treat lessening her nausea. It was a tangible, touchable, here-now reason for joy. Barrington was so kind, thinking of her discomfort when he had been so badly beaten.

Her heart trembled, which led to shaking palms. Barr was alive, sleeping upstairs in her chambers. Not dead, not missing. He was lucky. They were lucky.

Mama touched her face, fingering Amora's cheek with the butter soft leather of her gloves. "You have days, a few more months to figure everything out. But you will come together for this babe. You will figure out a path. Family is everything. It is stronger than a stubborn a la mula."

Footfalls pounded, coming closer.

Her pulse ticked. She tried to seem aloof, wiping a golden stain from her fingertips while peering toward the hall. The armor around her heart had to remain intact. Wanting Barrington would make her vulnerable to his opinions again. How long would it take for her to wilt under his practiced glare?

Mrs. Gretling pranced forward, whipping her rags as if they were on fire. She stopped at the entry. "Mrs. Norton, Mrs. Tomàs, I'm late going off to the foundlings. Sure you both don't want to come? The change will do you both good."

Lost in her fretting, Amora shook her head. Her spirit needed to settle. With Miller in the basement and Barr hurt, she couldn't lose her wits. She patted Mama's fingers then slipped again behind the safety of her easel. "Mr. Norton hasn't been feeling well. I'll stay and look after him. Mama's off to Cheapside."

"Yes, Mrs. Norton. The children miss ye." Mrs. Gretling shuffled down the hall.

She did miss the Foundling children. Her heart was filled with love for them and Jackson and Rebecca. She could touch them and see them laugh...and watch them breathe. She smoothed her smock over her small stomach. Was there hope for own?

The brass knocker sounded on the front door.

Mrs. Gretling pivoted and headed to the entry. "James is running errands for the master. I think he's at the optician since he's already delivered your morning ice."

A set of boot heels clicked along the polished planks. She pushed at a falling tendril hiding her disappointment that the noise wasn't coming from the stairs. Barrington still hadn't risen.

Samuel poked his head inside the parlor. "Morning, ladies. Well, well the master painter is at her craft. Rebecca will be sorry to have missed seeing your technique."

Mama headed to the mantle and pushed her Isis idol

closer to the garniture vases. "She is quite good. Maybe you with your silliness can get a peek."

With a hand on his deep indigo waistcoat, he sauntered to the easel. He whipped up her painting before Amora could stop him. "You are quite the artist. It looks like a spot I've seen in Clanville. Where is it? Oh, it will come to me."

"No, Vicar. That's the park we visited. Vaux Hall."

His forehead wrinkled. His countenance reddened with questions. "No, this is Clanville. I'm almost positive."

She came to his side, staring at the painting for a long time. It was familiar. She took her brush, dipped it into umber oil and feathered a shadow. Within an outline of her dark paint, a hidden structure became visible with her painted tree line. What was it?

Something unlocked in her mind. Images of that day, that moment she was taken, started to flow.

"Amora, what is it? You're shaking."

She heard her mother's voice, but couldn't respond. The images were too strong. She fisted her hands and poised to fight. The monster wouldn't take her this time.

"Sweetheart." Her mother clasped her wrists. "Why are you painting the Priory?"

In unison, Samuel and Amora repeated, "Priory."

Was that it? Not Vaux Hall?

Samuel eased the canvas back onto her easel. "Do you want to talk about it?"

Her heart beat an uneven, wobbly gait. She lowered her arms. "I don't."

She swished her brush in her small cup of water and watched the color bleed from the bristles. As if she didn't already know Mother's intended destination, she asked,

"How many warehouses will you visit today?"

Mama faked a smile, but her cheek held a tick. "The vicar has agreed to take me to as many as he can manage without falling into complaints." She fished into her reticule and produced a piece of foolscap in her hand. "Mr. Norton has requested some decorative items. Him, Mr. Dove gray asking for color."

Mama's delight for decorating should be infectious, but Amora kept painting, kept thinking of the Priory and how she had painted the ancient monastery the day she was abducted, as well. What could be the reason for that?

Too focused on stippling her brush strokes to unlock her unanswered question. Was this where the monster took her?

As if Samuel understood her unease, he held out his arm. "Come along, Mrs. Tomàs. Let's leave the artist to her work. I'm sure there are dozens of fabric warehouses calling for your presence. The children are well ensconced with my housekeeper, so nothing shall keep us from miles of embellishments."

"Go on, Mama. All will be well." That had to be true. That hope had to stay inside her, keeping the baby nourished and safe.

Samuel took her mother's hand and placed it about his forearm, wrinkling the midnight-blue sleeve of his tailcoat. "Well, Mrs. Tomàs, I'll even take you to an apothecary and suffer through your selection of weeds."

"Such a funny man, you obviously do not understand nature or the need for comfortable appointments for rooms."

"Like false gods? Or notions that make one depend on wooden things?" Samuel asked his questions with a lilt. It almost made his sarcasm palatable.

Mama bristled, but lifted her chin and headed to the door. "Come along, Vicar. Amora, take this time in a quiet house to talk with Mr. Norton."

The vicar shrugged as his smile grew. "She is right about a few things. If you won't talk to me, talk to him."

Samuel and Mama left. The door closed softly behind their gentle squabble. Quiet overtook the lower level. Only the swishing of Amora's brush against the side of her cup sounded, that and the noises of her broken memories. She'd been painting the Priory when the monster came.

Recognition fired her brainbox. She gasped. The Priory! The old Norman relic stashed at the edge of the forest. Was that where she'd been held? Yes. That was it. Peeling off her muslin smock, she headed to the hall. Barrington had to know immediately.

Clang, clang! Someone wrapped the knocker on the front door. It couldn't be Mama or Mrs. Gretling. They'd push inside. Her breathing hitched, shaking her loose grip on her nerves. Could it be Mr. Beakes coming to take Barrington away?

Amora hugged herself even as she chastised her weak thinking. Cowardice wouldn't save brave Barrington. It hadn't found her lost friend Sarah either. No, weak thinking had cost her too much.

Leveling her shoulders, she marched to the entry. Hiding quaking palms, she opened the door.

She groaned inwardly. Not her. Anybody but her.

Cynthia Miller stood there twisting her reticule along her finger. "May I come in?"

Before Amora could slam the door, Cynthia stuck her fingers into the door jamb. "Please. I came to see you.

You're my only hope."

The woman slithered inside. Sedate, in a heavy onyx drape, her dress wasn't alluring or colorful. Why was she dressed as if she was in mourning?

When had she ever done anything without causing a show? "What show is this for? Mr. Norton isn't feeling well enough for your shenanigans."

"I'm here to beg. I need to know where my brother is. Surely, you can help me."

The woman was mad, simply mad. Why should Amora do anything for the strumpet who'd tormented her these past few years? The woman whose lurid presence tainted Barrington's pristine reputation. Ignoring her own part in the debacle, she focused on the anger pulsing, fisting within her chest. "Harlot, get out of my house."

Eyes widening, Cynthia wrung her hands then drew a handkerchief out of her flopping reticule. "I am sorry. So very sorry. I know I have no right to ask—"

"Then why are you here? You're not my friend."

"Gloat. Slap me." She took Amora's hand and put it to her jaw. "Do it. Then tell me where Gerald is."

So tempted to drawback and let every ounce of her frustration discharge through her fingertips in the world's loudest slap, Amora broke free. A laugh bubbled out of her lips. "You love to play the victim. Bat your emerald eyes or toss a pouty look, and you expect the world to do your bidding. I know real victims. You do a disservice to them all."

"You suffered once, and then everything was restored to you. I suffer all the time."

Seething, uncaring of the height disadvantage, Amora marched to her. "What do you mean?"

Cynthia bit her lip. "I was talking about your being separated from Barrington for so long. That's all." She closed her palm as if she protected something. "I've had to seize every opportunity to better my station. I snatched up what I could get."

Amora's stomach turned. She clenched her fingers. The vixen had known of her abduction all this time. How?

The singer stormed past her, whipping into the parlor. Bright red tendrils spilled from her chignon as her gaze settled onto the new painting.

The woman pivoted. Tears dribbled down her rouged cheeks. "I just want to see my brother!"

There wasn't time to determine Cynthia's complicity with all the noise she made. Amora pointed to the door. "Miss Miller, leave."

"I'm not budging, not until Barrington tells me where he took Gerald. I know he stole him from Bedlam. What would happen to his reputation if that became known?"

"Yes, I wonder what would happen to my reputation?"

Cynthia's head jerked toward the hall. Her snide features melted away as her mouth fell open.

Barrington stood at the threshold. A crisp white shirt peeked from behind his onyx waistcoat. The fine silver threading of his vest reflected candlelight, giving his muscled frame radiance.

A wince showed on his lean cheek as he folded his powerful arms. "I suppose Gerald and I will share a cell at Newgate, but he won't be there for long. He'll hang for the murder of a Clanville milkmaid, Nan Druby."

Eyes wide, the woman gasped as she looked at Barrington. "What happened to you?"

The dark blue circle along his jaw made him seem

battle-hardened, impervious to anything. He tweaked the metal rims of his new glasses, sliding them further upon his nose. "It's of no consequence. Go and spread your truth or lies to the magistrate. Make sure to tell how you know Miller didn't strangle Nan Druby."

"Gerald didn't kill her or anyone." Sobbing, Cynthia rushed close to Barrington. "I'd never hurt you. I'm just in anguish over not knowing where my brother is."

He side-stepped her as if she had leprosy. "Leave now as my wife commanded or prepare to watch Miller swing at Debtor's Door. At least with the white hood covering his face before the execution, you won't see the look of betrayal in his eyes."

She backed up to Amora and dumped guineas into her palm. "Use this and put him on a ship to Australia or the Americas, somewhere they won't find him. I'll go with him, too. Amora, you'll never see me again. That should make you happy."

Done with trying to keep her temper restrained, Amora tossed the money back at her, sending the singer scrambling for the bouncing coins. "The truth must reign, no matter what. I know that now. Leave my home, leave my marriage and be gone!"

Barrington leaned against the doorframe, his split lip curled up. "You heard Mrs. Norton."

The vixen spun and stormed to the door. "I'll never forgive you, any of you."

Cynthia left. Her slam of the door shook the hall sconces, causing the light to flicker, but none lost its flame. Amora hadn't either. Getting closer to the truth girded her.

Barrington held out his hand to her. "Well, let's see what my formerly dead friend has to say."

Amora pivoted. She squinted at him. "Formerly dead or formerly your friend?"

He wrenched the back of his neck, his gaze pinned on her new canvas. "Well, he's breathing now. Come along."

Chapter Ten: Finding the Past

Barrington gripped her hand, filled his aching lungs and opened the cellar door. He dreaded this moment. "I don't suppose there is a way I can dissuade you from coming?"

Her eyes held determination. Her chin lifted as she towed him forward. "No."

It wasn't a good idea to take her downstairs.

It wasn't good that his palm warmed holding onto hers.

It wasn't good that she'd witness him ripping at his friend or killing him if he harmed a hair on her head.

He dragged to a halt, his low heels digging into the last tread. "How can you be so sure of Miller's innocence? You don't remember the whole of it. You've suppressed the events."

She poked him in the chest right above his bandages. "What are you not telling me, Barrington?"

He shrugged and kept moving until they reached the door. His heart pounded as he took the knob, but he couldn't turn it. "What if all your memories return and you become strained. We could avoid this if you don't hear Miller's testimony?"

Her lips pursed. There was fire in her eyes. "Barrington Norton always seeks the truth. Why not now?"

How could she not understand what his quest for truth had already cost? What it could cost them? He took her hand within his and almost pressed them against her abdomen. "I won't let this man hurt you. I'm supposed to protect you."

"I'll be fine." She kept their hands linked, but used her other hand to open the door. "The truth must reign. No more secrets. I can't live with any more secrets."

As he followed her inside, he couldn't quite agree. Denial looked pretty good right now.

Dressed in a pair of James's old liveries, Gerald sat up. The faded blue jacket swallowed the man. His eyes seemed so vacant within the rag thin face. "Norton. Didn't do it."

Barrington eased Amora onto a stool. He lifted his arm anchoring his fingers to the revers of his waistcoat. "Miller, let's start with how you are alive. I saw you take the bullet that was headed for me. I witnessed you fall, the blood oozing from your chest. Before I could give you aid, another blast ate into my hip. I couldn't get to you."

Gerald worked his gums. His lips twitched before he said, "Yes."

The affirmation sounded weak and soon evaporated in the quiet. A quiet that surrounded Barrington with the noises of that awful morning in the Peninsula.

Cannons fired in the distance.

Grunts and yells of fallen comrades whipped up and

down in the fast wind. The scent of butchered flesh, torn off limbs, and death smelled fresh.

"I saw..." His voice broke. "I saw them cart your body off before losing consciousness. Gerald, you saved my life. You were dead, all for saving me."

"Yes, Nor-ton."

His hands shook with frustration, Norton planted his feet inches from the bed. "It was a torment to know you died in my stead. Why induce such mourning to my soul? Why didn't you find me?"

His friend blinked and licked his pale lips. "Yes."

Miller's tone was soft, babe-like. "Yes. Shot." He tapped his shoulders and pried open his shirt, exposing a bullet wound. "Woke in farmhouse. B-Before burial. I fled."

Amora sat at the edge of the stool. Though her countenance was smooth, she rocked a little as if impatient. Well, Barrington thought, she had her own truth to hunt.

He shifted his stance to keep his feet from scooping her and taking her far from here. He couldn't. She needed her answers more than anything else. "Miller, why didn't you come back to camp? The colonel might have sent you home anyway."

"Cynthia. Fam-ily need me." Gerald coughed and shook his thin frame. "Only one to help."

Though he could understand protecting his family, a harsh sigh seeped from Barrington. "You could've found me, sent word somehow. The day still haunts me."

A soft palm gripped his tight fist. He jerked, realizing too late that it was Amora.

"I didn't know you harbored such feelings. You could've shared them with me." She held onto his clenched fingers.

He couldn't respond. How does a man tell of his nightmares? And even if he could, what happens when his wife's were darker?

She released him and edged to the bed. "Mr. Miller, tell him about finding me."

His friend lay back and flung an arm over his head, as if the candlelight pained his eyes. He rocked for a moment then settled. "The aches. They come, go."

Impatient, Barrington paced. His low heels knocked an uneven gait against the floor. "Upon slinking back from the war, how did you find my fiancée and Miss Druby?"

Gerald struggled for a breath, shaking. He puckered his mouth and wrinkled his brow. "Hate me because I deserted?"

Hate wasn't what stewed in his gut. The thick stew turning and twisting inside was guilt. Miller followed him to the war. If Barrington hadn't been seeking additional ways to please his grandfather, he would never have agreed to enlistment. Miller wouldn't be in this trouble and Barrington would not have left Amora unprotected.

He wiped his hands along his waistcoat, but the guilt remained on his palms, thick and sticky. "I loved you like a brother, Miller. I would've gladly taken that bullet. But if you hurt my wife, nothing will keep me from breaking you with my own hands."

"Never. Never hurt. I found."

"Where, Mr. Miller?" Amora gripped the sides of the bed. Her fingertips dug into the mattress.

Gerald coughed, reached for a mug and sipped. "Dark place with creaking floorboards."

Barrington froze. Every abandoned or seldom-rented

house of Clanville crammed his skull. "Was it an old cottage?"

Gerald shrugged. His gaze locked upon Amora. "I heard her below."

Unable to stop himself, Barrington seized the lapels of his friend's coat and raised him up. The mug flew from Gerald's hands, sprinkling water everywhere, but mostly on Barrington's new spectacles. "You heard Amora? Was she crying?"

"No. Told my Nan, refuse...the beast."

Barrington closed his eyes and released him. "My brave girl. Then what?"

Gerald slouched against a pillow. His face became more ashen. "Couldn't pull off the chains."

Barrington braced against the wall. "You left her? How—"

"I told him to." Amora's small voice penetrated his soul. "It was Nan's turn. The monster was coming for her that night. She'd agreed to do whatever he wished. She'd agreed... It was the only way to be re...released."

Her words had drowned within her quiet sobs, but she wiped her chin and stood up straight. "The monster made each girl consent to his depravity. Then he'd take them away. He took Sarah. I still hear her screams some nights."

That is what Hessing's notes said of the Dark Walk Abductor's victims. Charred fury filled Barrington, constricting his lungs, gripping and breaking the restraint he'd mastered all his life. He leaned back against the wall, hoping not to punch at the limestone and break his hand.

He forced air in and out of his mouth, but nothing could rob him of the image of Amora being humbled by her monster. Amora had to be one of the Dark Walk Abductor's victims. Would she survive knowing all of the truth?

Would the baby?

With a deep sigh, Gerald sat up, his thin legs dangled over the edge of the bed. "Didn't do it. Believe me."

Gerald's tone sounded honest, but was that just Barrington's broken spirit listening, hearing things that salved his soul?

Anything had to be better than imagining her screaming from too early of a quickening, of her crying over another child lost.

Barrington put a hand to his neck. The vein on the side pulsed. "Is it your testimony that Miss Druby was alive when you freed her? That you never took her or helped any other do this evil?"

Gerald's large eyes widened. He stared in Barrington's direction. "Yes." A clear, strong announcement.

The man spoke the truth. Barrington felt it in his bones. A piece of his heart glued back into place. His beloved friend wasn't the monster or in league with the monster. Thank God. "What happened to you?"

Gerald lowered to the bed. "Big man. I fought him, ripped his coat." He closed his fist as if he held something in it, then lowered his arm to the mattress. "Ripped a button. Bricks dropped on me."

"He's a victim, too." Amora's face pivoted toward the ceiling. She wasn't crying, but chanting. She said, "Bricks. Brick falling."

His gut ached to pull her into his arms, but she needed to sort through her memories without him coddling her, depriving her of strength. Yet, Barrington's skull burned with questions. "If Gerald didn't free you, how did you escape? Do you remember?"

Amora looked so distant, everything inside him broke again.

"I don't know, Barr."

Someone opened the chains on her pen. If it wasn't Miller, then the abductor did. Barrington ran a hand through his hair and walked over to Amora. All the other women were released after being abused. Was that Amora's fate? Was that why she couldn't remember?

Barrington knelt before his wife, took her palm and placed it against the rapid beats of his chest. "What did he do to you?"

She closed her eyes. "I don't know. I hear the screams. Bricks falling all around."

Her eyelids popped open. She grabbed his waistcoat. "Footsteps pounded behind me. His voice was low as he cursed. I was to blame for what he did to Nan. He hit me and I fell against an altar... Altar?"

Forget the chasm between them. She needed his strength. He scooped her up until her trembling ceased. "I knew this was a bad idea. 'Tis too much for you."

"Not if it means I can see the clues hidden in my mind." She pushed at his chest and stepped free, almost leaping to Miller. "I was painting the Priory the day I was taken. Did you find me at the Priory?"

That old Norman relic? The Priory sat near Grandfather's lands. Barrington swiped at his brow. "The dilapidated monastery at...at the edge of Norton property? We used to play in that thing as children. Miller, think, man. You're the only one to confirm where she and the others were held."

Gerald opened his mouth then closed it. He punched his head. "Don't know."

Barrington grabbed his hands and stilled them against the mattress. "Easy, my friend. You've given us enough."

The bosom buddy of his youth turned his sorrow-filled eyes toward Barrington. It felt like a sword in his gut, tearing at his conscience for doubting him. "Then, you believe...me."

"Yes, I do. When I find the monster, it will prove your innocence. I'll help you get your life back."

A small smile formed on Gerald's face as his eyes dimmed.

"Rest, Miller. The villain's face might come to you. You're the only one who can say."

Amora looked at Gerald then toward the doorway. She ran.

Barrington scampered after her praying she wouldn't trip on the stair treads. "Sweetheart, wait!"

She pounded onto the main floor.

Where was she going? Was she in pain? He struggled up the final step, his hip aching with each footfall. He had to catch her, had to reason with her before something tragic happened. "Wait!"

His wife, his heart, pivoted from the main threshold and slid into the parlor. By the time he got to her, she stood frozen in front of her easel. Placid, with her arms folded, her gaze seemed transfixed upon the canvas.

With slow careful steps, he approached her and put his hands upon her shoulders. His fingers falling into the soft lilac capped sleeves of her gown. "Whatever you are remembering, we can face it together."

"There is one who knows. Sarah. The woman in Bedlam the vicar told us about. If she is my friend, she'll be able to tell you where we were held. She can give you proof if my monster is the Dark Walk Abductor."

Barrington pulled her against him, letting her sink against his bruised ribs. He needed her to be there, the pain bridging a path to her. She couldn't slip away from him now, not with everything in jeopardy. "Sarah Calloway's in Bedlam. She may not be able to say anything useful because of her madness. She could be a danger to you."

"I have to know. I need proof. Surely, we need to know for certain if my monster is the Dark Walk Abductor."

He spun her from her painting, forcing her to look at his face. Couldn't she see his concerns for her? He put his palms on her cheeks. His heart ripped open, bursting with the need to protect her from all the darkness of the world, from her addled memories. "We can't risk it. Not now."

"For the babe's sake. I know that's your concern, Barrington—"

"We don't need any more proof. I believe you. I know you were one of his victims. Isn't that enough?"

A single tear flopped onto her lashes. Another trickled along her delicate nose. "I don't know, though. And if the fear he left inside me stays, he'll win. Your love, God's keeping, it isn't enough to keep me fighting, not if I have questions taunting me in the dark."

She reached out, fisted her hand around a button on his waistcoat. "Help me go to her. Help me win."

Against his better judgment, he gave into the hurt look filling her violet eyes. She needed to conquer this, and it would only come by her standing strong and facing Sarah. "Yes. I'll take you to see her."

She swept her arms around his neck. He tried to memorize the feel of her, her wanting him and coming to him. Once Amora understood all she and the others had suffered, this gentle warrior would disappear. She'd be engulfed in the madness that consumed all of the victims of the Dark Walk Abductor.

And Barrington would be alone, knowing he'd destroyed his wife and babe by giving Amora what she desired.

Please Leave A Review

If you like these stories, please leave a review.

I love being able to write these books. I hope you love them too. As an author, I depend on you, the reader, to get the word out about my books. If you liked this book, please leave a review online and recommend it to a friend. The more you spread the word, the more books I can write and nothing would please me more than to create more of these stories for you.

Thank you.

Vanessa Riley

Sneak Peek: Episode IV

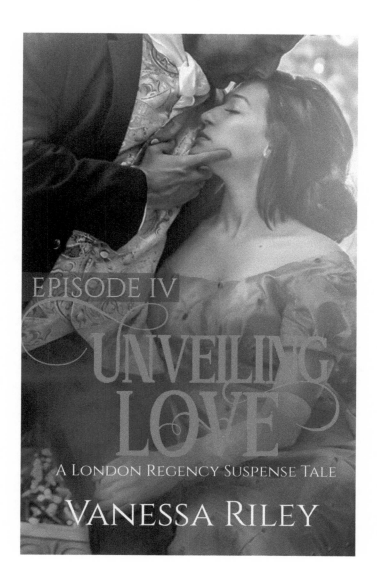

EPISODE IV

UNVEILING
LOVE

A LONDON REGENCY SUSPENSE TALE

VANESSA RILEY

Episode IV of Unveiling Love
Length: 9 Chapters (35,000 words)
Summary: Season Finale

Amora Norton needs to make all the victims of the Dark Walk Abductor truth-tellers. And she will risk all, her health and her heart, to see justice. She now understands she'll never have peace until everything is made known. Yet, will she survive disappointing Barrington one final time?

Barrington Norton refuses to lose one more thing and will stop Amora from risking her life to catch a killer. This barrister will take it upon himself to protect her and will sentence the monster who has stolen everything Barrington values. Nonetheless, is he willing to pay the ultimate price to make his wife whole?

Pre-order/order the next Episode which releases April 2016. Join my newsletter to stay informed and if you liked this please leave a review.

Here's your sneak peek at the next episode.

If you like these stories, please leave a review.

I love being able to write these books. I hope you love them too. As an author, I depend on you, the reader, to get the word out about my books. If you liked this book, please leave a review online and recommend it to a friend. The more you spread the word, the more books I can write and nothing would please me more than to create more of these stories for you.

Thank you.

Vanessa Riley

Sneak Peak: Episode IV copy

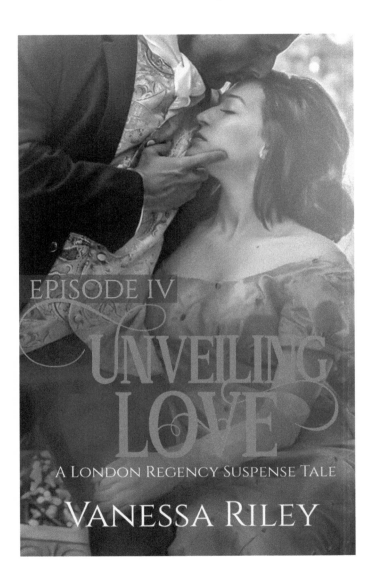

EPISODE IV

UNVEILING
LOVE

A LONDON REGENCY SUSPENSE TALE

VANESSA RILEY

Episode IV of Unveiling Love
Length: 9 Chapters (35,000 words)
Summary: Season Finale

Amora Norton needs to make all the victims of the
Dark Walk Abductor truth-tellers. And she will risk all,
her health and her heart, to see justice. She now
understands she'll never have peace until everything is
made known. Yet, will she survive disappointing
Barrington one final time?

Barrington Norton refuses to lose one more thing and
will stop Amora from risking her life to catch a killer.
This barrister will take it upon himself to protect her and
will sentence the monster who has stolen everything
Barrington values. Nonetheless, is he willing to pay the
ultimate price to make his wife whole?

Pre-order/order the next Episode which releases April 2016. Join my newsletter to stay informed and if you liked this please leave a review.

Here's your sneak peek at the next episode.

Chapter One: Finding Sarah

Amora took Barrington's hand and allowed his strong arms to help her down from his carriage. Her gaze fell upon the stone walls surrounding Bedlam. It took a week for Barrington and Samuel to coerce Mr. Calloway's permission. A whole seven days of trying to find things to paint, of pretending not to notice Barrington's goings and comings from the attic, or his wincing as his wound was dressed.

None of this distracted her. Only the hope of seeing Sarah kept her wits level.

James doffed his hat to her and bounced back to his post atop the carriage. "Happy hunting, sir and madam."

His man's soulful eyes told his heart. He must be concerned about his master returning to Bedlam.

James leaned his head down. His gaze locked onto Barrington's. "I'll be ready to leave at a moment's notice."

Her husband nodded. "Thank you."

Barrington took her hand and led her through the courtyard. His posture hunched as if weighted by all the heaviness of the world. Perhaps his hip still bothered him. A week from being nearly beaten to death wasn't enough time to heal.

She stopped, reached up and adjusted his cravat, fluffing the folds of the bright white lawn fabric. "This will go well."

He clasped her hand and looked down upon her. His silvery gray eyes seemed so distant. No crinkles formed of humor, just harsh lines from lack of sleep, or worse, fear. "It's not too late." His tone was low. It bordered upon desperate. "We can get an ice. Do anything else, but this."

Fingers intertwined, he pressed closer, folding her within his strong embrace. His lips slipped to her brow. "We could leave London forever. We could travel. We could see the world. Let me give you the world."

He'd only begged once in his life that she'd witnessed and that was the day she tried to toss herself off the cliff in Clanville.

Was that it?

Did he assume she'd lose her reason knowing the truth? Couldn't he see it was the only way to keep her wits? She brought her dark indigo gloved hands to his chin. "The truth will set us free. Trust in me, please."

His gray eyes darted. His lips pressed into a firmer line. Surely, he couldn't pledge to completely trust in her. It wasn't in him to lie.

But she had faith in herself. It might be small and mangled, but it was hers. She could not rest not knowing, not anymore. Only the truth could save her.

They plodded up the stairs. Barrington held open the door and allowed her inside. The stench of mustard and tonics wafted down the corridor. She put a hand to her nose. The place was dark.

Barrington tugged his hat off. He trudged back and forth waiting. "The caregiver, Mr. Greene, will be here soon."

He stopped by a door and touched the handle. "To think, Miller was here all that time. I could've visited him if Miss Miller had been honest."

"Those words don't seem to go together, Miss Miller and honesty."

A tall grim-faced man cleaning his large onyx spectacles appeared at the entrance of the long hall.

Barrington walked over to him and shook his hand. "I'm Barrister Norton. You're Mr. Greene?"

"That I am." He tweaked his thick mustache. "The head administrator of Bethlehem Hospital. I understand you want to see Miss Calloway. It's getting a bit late in the evening for visiting."

Barrington nodded. His fingers fumbled along the brim of his top hat. "Miss Calloway is a potential witness to a crime. She's one of the Dark Walk Abductor's victim."

"Crying shame what they say happened."

Like awakening from a fog, Barrington stepped forward. His grip tightened on his hat, almost as if thumbs would pierce the fabric. "It did happen. We just don't know who the villain is."

"Well, let's see if the woman is not so dour tonight." Waving, Mr. Greene led them down a long hall. "Miss Calloway disappeared from Vaux Hall and was found a month later, babbling in a ditch a few hours outside of London. Horrible condition."

A few hours? Amora thought. That could be Clanville, couldn't it? If this woman was Sarah, then Barrington was right. Amora swallowed. How much would her world change knowing that the Dark Walk Abductor held her captive?

Voices echoed.

Unintelligible mumblings seemed to crowd them as they paced deeper into the building. A darkened room of beds and bodies lay to the right.

Greene trudged past, head held high as if the patients were part of the wall. How could one grow cold to human misery?

The administrator's snow covered head stopped bobbing in front of an illuminated door. It stood apart in the dim passageway, the only one with light pouring from the frame.

Barrington's countenance dimmed. "She needs a great deal of light even in the evenings when she should be sleeping?"

Greene huffed, as if the burden to not be overtaken by darkness was something one could help. "Miss Calloway is quiet if we keep her room lit." He pulled out a skeleton key from his long coat and pressed it into the lock.

As Amora followed, the smells of urine and stale air assaulted her. The familiar toxic perfume wrenched at her soul. Oh, how she'd rather smell the stinging scent of lye soap from the asylum or even wretched chrysanthemums. Her fingers trembled. She stuffed her hands into her pockets.

A lump with blonde hair rolled into a ball was chained to the bed. Attached to the plain grey wall were two make shift wall sconces. Large candles burned from above. If the candles snuffed, the poor girl and everyone in the room wouldn't see more than a few inches forward. Amora's heart raced. Being trapped in this small space with no light would be death.

Extras

Author's Note

Dear Friend,

I enjoyed writing Unveiled Love because diverse Regency London needs its story told, and I am a sucker for a wonderful husband and wife romance. They need love after the vows, too.

These stories will showcase a world of intrigue and romance, a setting everyone can hopefully find a character to identify with in the battle of love, which renews and gives life.

Stay in touch. Sign up at www.vanessariley.com for my newsletter. You'll be the first to know about upcoming releases, and maybe even win a sneak peek.

Thank so much for giving this book a read.

Vanessa Riley

Many of my readers are new to Regencies, so I always

add notes and a glossary to make items readily available. If you know of a term that should be added to enhance my readers' knowledge, send them to me at: vanessa@christianregency.com. I will acknowledge you in my next book.

Here are my notes:

Mulatto Barristers

I couldn't find definitive proof of one, but that does not mean it was impossible. Connections and success bent rules. Such was the case for William Garrow (1760-1840). He was not born a gentleman and didn't go to the best schools. Yet, his success in the courts rewrote how trials would be performed. He introduced the premise, "presumed innocent until proven guilty," and rose to become Solicitor General for England and Wales.

Free blacks in 1800's English Society

By Regency times, historians, Kirstin Olsen and Gretchen Holbrook Gerzina, estimate that Black London (the black neighborhood of London) had over 10,000 residents. While England led the world in granting rights to the enslaved and ending legal slavery thirty years before the American Civil War, it still had many citizens who were against change. Here is another image from an anti-abolitionist.

The New Union Club being a representation of what took place at a celebrated dinner given by a celebrated society – includes in picture abolitionists, Billy Waters, Zachariah Macauley, William Wilberforce. – published 19 July 1819. Source: Wiki Commons

The NEW UNION-CLUB

Notable People Mentioned in this Serial

William Wilberforce (1759-1833) was an abolitionist who sought to end England's slave trade which existed within the Empire's colonies. His conversion to Evangelical Christianity made him change his outlook on life and to seek reform.

Zachary Macaulay (1768-1838) was an abolitionist and a former governor of Sierra Leone. Like Wilberforce, his faith drove him to try to end the slave trade.

George Bridgetower (George Augustus Polgreen Bridgetower) was born in Poland on October 11, 1778. The mulatto described as Afro-European was the son of John Frederick Bridgetower, a West Indie's black man and a white German maid. He became a virtuoso violinist whose talents were recognized by the Prince Regent. The prince took an interest in his education and directed Bridgetower's musical studies. Bridgetower performed in many concerts in London theatres like,

Covent Garden, Drury Lane and the Haymarket Theatre. In the spring of 1789, Bridgetower performed at the Abbaye de Panthemont in Paris. Thomas Jefferson attended this event. Bridgewater died February 1860.

Harriet Westbrook was the first wife of Percy Shelley. She was abandoned by Lord Shelley when he fell in love with **Mary Wollstonecraft.** On 10 December 1816, Harriet's body was found. She was pregnant when she was drowned in the the Serpentine in Hyde Park, London.

King George III, the king who lost the American colonies, suffered from bouts of mental illness. His son ruled in his stead as the Prince Regent (George Augustus Frederick). King George III died January 27, 1820. Mourning for a King had three parts: deep mourning (eight weeks), mourning (two weeks), and half-mourning (two weeks). During these times, clothing and accessories had to be correlated to the type of mourning.

Inter-racial marriages occurred.

The children known as mulattos lived lives on the scale of their education and wealth. Examine this painting. Portrait of a Mulatto by FABRE, François-Xavier. It is from 1809-1810. Portraits were indicative to status and wealth. My screenshot of the image the art once displayed at Arenski Fine Art, LTD London. More information can be found at http://maryrobinettekowal.com/journal/images-of-regency-era-free-people-of-colour/.

This painting of an interracial couple and child, *Pintura de Castas*, from Spaniard and Mulatto, Morisca (1763). Where love exists barriers fade.

Slavery in England

The emancipation of slaves in England preceded America by thirty years and freedom was won by legal court cases not bullets.

Somerset v Stewart (1772) is a famous case, which established the precedence for the rights of slaves in England. The English Court of King's Bench, led by Lord Mansfield, decided that slavery was unsupported by the common law of England and Wales. His ruling:

"The state of slavery is of such a nature that it is incapable of being introduced on any reasons, moral or political, but only by positive law, which preserves its force long after the reasons, occasions, and time itself from whence it was created, is erased from memory. It is so odious, that nothing can be suffered to support it, but positive law. Whatever inconveniences, therefore, may follow from the decision, I cannot say this case is allowed or approved by the law of England; and therefore the black must be discharged."

E. Neville William, The Eighteenth-Century Constitution: 1688-1815, pp: 387-388.

The Slavery Abolition Act 1833 was an act of Parliament, which abolished slavery throughout the British Empire. A fund of $20 Million Pound Sterling was set up to compensate slave owners. Many of the highest society families were compensated for losing their slaves.

This act did exempt the territories in the possession of the East India Company, the Island of Ceylon, and the Island of Saint Helena. In 1843, the exceptions were eliminated.

Glossary

The Regency – The Regency is a period of history from 1811-1825 (sometimes expanded to 1795-1837) in England. It takes its name from the Prince Regent who ruled in his father's stead when the king suffered mental illness. The Regency is known for manners, architecture, and elegance. Jane Austen wrote her famous novel, *Pride and Prejudice* (1813), about characters living during the Regency.

England is a country in Europe. London is the capital city of England.

Image of England from a copper engraved map created by William Darton in 1810.

Port Elizabeth was a town founded in 1820 at the tip of South Africa. The British settlement was an attempt to strengthen England's hold on the Cape Colony and to be a buffer from the Xhosa.

Xhosa - A proud warrior people driven to defend their land and cattle-herding way of life from settlers expanding the boundaries of the Cape Colony.

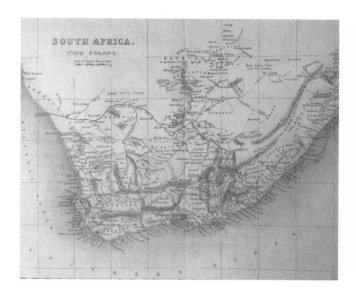

Image of South Africa from a copper engraved map created by John Dower in 1835.

Abigail – A lady's maid.

Soiree – An evening party.

Bacon-brained – A term meaning foolish or stupid.

Black – A description of a black person or an African.

Black Harriot – A famous prostitute stolen from Africa, then brought to England by a Jamaican planter who died, leaving her without means. She turned to harlotry to earn a living. Many members of the House of Lords became her clients. She is described as tall, genteel, and alluring, with a degree of politeness.

Blackamoor – A dark-skinned person.

Bombazine – Fabric of twilled or corded cloth made of silk and wool or cotton and wool. Usually the material was dyed black and used to create mourning clothes.

Breeched – The custom of a young boy no longer wearing pinafores and now donning breeches. This occurs about age six.

Breeches – Short, close-fitting pants for men, which fastened just below the knees and were worn with stockings.

Caning – A beating typically on the buttocks for naughty behavior.

Compromise – To compromise a reputation is to ruin or cast aspersions on someone's character by catching them with the wrong people, being alone with someone who wasn't a relative at night, or being caught doing something wrong. During the Regency, gentlemen were often forced to marry women they had compromised.

Dray – Wagon.

Footpads – Thieves or muggers in the streets of London.

Greatcoat – A big outdoor overcoat for men.

Mews – A row of stables in London for keeping horses.

Pelisse - An outdoor coat for women that is worn over a dress.

Quizzing Glass – An optical device, similar to a monocle, typically worn on a chain. The wearer might use the quizzing glass to look down upon people.

Reticule – A cloth purse made like a bag that had a drawstring closure.

Season – One of the largest social periods for high society in London. During this time, a lady attended a variety of balls and soirees to meet potential mates.

Sideboard – A low piece of furniture the height of a writing desk, which housed spirits.

Ton – Pronounced *tone*, the *ton* was a high class in society during the Regency era.

Sneak Peak: Unmasked Heart

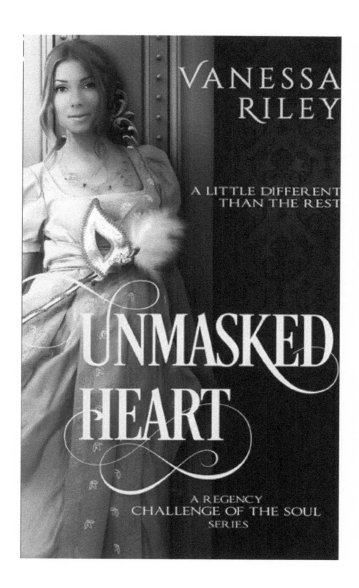

VANESSA
RILEY

A LITTLE DIFFERENT
THAN THE REST

UNMASKED
HEART

A REGENCY
CHALLENGE OF THE SOUL
SERIES

Shy, nearsighted caregiver, Gaia Telfair always wondered why her father treated her a little differently than her siblings, but she never guessed she couldn't claim his love because of a family secret, her illicit birth. With everything she knows to be true evaporating before her spectacles, can the mulatto passing for white survive being exposed and shunned by the powerful duke who has taken an interest in her?

Ex-warrior, William St. Landon, the Duke of Cheshire, will do anything to protect his mute daughter from his late wife's scandals. With a blackmailer at large, hiding in a small village near the cliffs of Devonshire seems the best option, particularly since he can gain help from the talented Miss Telfair, who has the ability to help children learn to speak. If only he could do a better job at shielding his heart from the young lady, whose honest hazel eyes see through his jests as her tender lips challenge his desire to remain a single man.

Unmasked Heart is the first Challenge of the Soul Regency novel.

Excerpt from Unmasked Heart: The Wrong Kiss

Seren adjusted the delicate gauzy silk flowers lining the edges of Gaia's cape. "Wait here until your Elliot arrives. Don't leave this room; I'll come back to find you."

Part of Gaia didn't want to release Seren's hand. Half-seeing things made the room frightening. Her pulse raced. "What if someone else arrives?"

"Tell them the room is occupied. They'll understand." Seren adjusted her silvery sarsenet cape, balanced the scales she hung on a cord in place of a reticule, and smoothed her wide skirts.

Grasping hold of the armrest, Gaia forced her lips to smile. "Good luck to you, Lady Justice. I hope you have fun."

"If you find the love you seek, I'll be happy. You deserve happiness for being you, not someone's daughter. Tell Elliot of your love. Gaia, you need a name and a household of your own, where secrets can't harm you." She gave Gaia a hug. "I want your cup filled with joy."

"Even if my cup isn't pure."

"Your heart is untainted by the past, made pure by salvation. That's what matters." Seren put a hand to Gaia's face. In the candlelight, she and Seren, their skin, looked the same. "Live free tonight."

Seren moved out of focus and left the room, closing the door behind her.

The lime blur of the settee was as comfortable as it was big, but Gaia couldn't sit still. She fidgeted and tapped her slippers on the floor. The ticking of the mantle clock filled the quiet room.

Trying to ignore it, she clutched the ribbons of her papier-mâché mask and straightened its creamy feathers. She stood and, with the pace of a turtle, she moved to the fireplace and strained to see where the limbs of timepiece pointed. Nine-fifteen.

Elliot would be here soon. What would she say to him? Would she remain silent and just dance with him?

She leveled her shoulders. How could she not say her peace, as she looked into his blue eyes? How ironic to unmask her heart at a masquerade ball.

The moon finally broke through the clouds and cast its light into the salon. Whether from the fuzziness of her vision or the beauty of the glow, the window glass sparkled, as did the mirrors and polished candleholders of the small room.

The low tones of the musicians started up again. The jaunty steps of a reel sounded. The tone called to her feet again, and she danced as if she were in someone's arms. The beechnut- colored walls and white moldings swirled as she did.

That set ended and then another and another. She paced in front of the mantle clock. It tolled a low moan as it struck ten. Elliot had missed their appointment. Heaviness weighed upon Gaia, from the crown of her costume's veils to the thick folds of her opal domino.

How ironic to stand in such finery, when Mr. Telfair told her she wasn't worthy. Yet hadn't she schemed with her stepmother and Seren to be here? Gaia should leave. Too many wrongs would never equal righteousness.

Movement outside the room sent her pulse racing. Maybe Elliot had been detained, but was still coming. She wrung her hands and looked to the shining circle on the door, its crystal knob.

The footsteps passed by, the sound diminishing, as did her dreams.

Elliot wouldn't show. He must still think of her as a child, as Julia's hapless sister, as Millicent's plain cousin. Or maybe Julia had told him. They could be laughing about it now.

Sighs and a misguided tear leaked out. She leaned against the burnished mantle. The warmth of the hearth did nothing to thaw her suddenly-cold feet. It was best he didn't show. He'd saved her the embarrassment of his rejection. A mulatto's dance or kiss could never do for him.

The rhythm of a dance set crept beneath the ivory doorframe. Maybe Elliot found a new young lady, whose large dowry like Millicent's made her irresistible to men. Was she in his arms, basking in the glow of his smile, his fun conversation?

The ache in her bosom swelled. Gaia released her breath, stilling her trembling fingers against the sheer veil of her fairy costume. Perhaps she should slip from the room and run into the moonlight of the moors.

The door opened. The strains of violin-play seeped into the salon.

Elliot in his domino cape and ebony half-mask entered the room. "Excuse me," his voice was low, hoarse. He whipped a handkerchief from his pocket and wiped his mouth as he bowed.

Always so formal, but what a pity his melodious voice sounded raspy.

Now or never. She cleared her throat and, in her most sultry manner, she placed her hands to her hips and curtsied. "I've been waiting for you."

"Excuse me, do I know you?" He tugged at the ribbons of his mask.

Waving her arms, she caught his gaze. "Please don't take it off. I won't be able to get through this if you expose your handsome face."

"I see." He stopped, his strong hands lowering beneath the cape of his domino. "Miss Telfair?"

With a quick motion, she whipped up her airy silk skirts and traipsed closer, but maintained an easy distance on the other side of the settee. "Call me Gaia.

We needn't be so formal."

His head moved from side-to-side, as if to scan the room.

"You needn't fret, sir. We are quite alone. That's why I decided to confess my feelings."

"I see."

Must he continue to act as if he didn't know her? The moonbeams streaming through the thick window mullions surrounded him, and reflected in the shiny black silk of his cape. Could he be taller, more intimidating?

Elliot had to think of her as a woman. She straightened her shoulders. "I'm so glad you've come. I know I'm young, but not too young to know my heart."

"Miss Telfair, I think this is some sort of mistake."

Blood pounding in her ears, she swept past the settee and stood within six feet of him. "Please call me Gaia."

"I'll not trespass on your privacy any longer." He spun, as if to flee.

She shortened the distance and caught his shoulder. "Please don't go. It took a lot to garner the courage to meet you here."

With a hesitance she'd never seen from confident Elliot, he gripped her palm and kissed her satin glove. "I know it takes a great amount of courage to make a fool of one's self."

"There's no better fool than one in love." She slipped his hand to her cheek. "Why hide behind mocking? I know you. I've seen your heart. The way you take care of that precious little girl as if she were your own." It touched Gaia, witnessing Elliot helping his brother's household as if it were his own.

"How did you know my fear?" He drew his hand to

his mouth. "You see too much."

Squinting, he still wasn't quite in focus. He shifted his weight and rubbed his neck, as if her compliments made him nervous.

"This is a mistake. We should forget this conversation. A man shouldn't be alone with such a forthright young lady. I will return to the ball." He leveled his broad shoulders and marched to the door, his heels clicking the short distance.

Maybe being so low was freeing. "Why leave?" she let her voice sound clear, no longer cautioned with shyness or regret. "Here can be no worse than out there, with the other ladies readying to weigh your pockets."

His feet didn't move, but he closed the door, slamming it hard. Had she struck a nerve?

He pivoted to face her. "Aren't you just like them, my dear? Weren't all gentle women instructed to follow a man's purse? No? Perhaps torturing is your suit, demanding more and more until nothing remains of his soul."

"Men hunt for dowries, and they know best how to torture someone; ignoring people who want their best; separating friends, even sisters, in their pursuits. The man who raised me did so begrudgingly, just to make me a governess to my brother. Is there no worse torture than to yearn to be loved and no one care?"

"A governess? I think I understand."

This wasn't how she'd expected this conversation to go. Elliot's graveled words possessed an edge as sharp as a sword. He seemed different, both strong and vulnerable. It must be the costumes, freeing them both from the confining roles they lived.

Yet he didn't move. He didn't feel the same.

She fanned her shimmering veil. Half-seeing and disguised, she could be as bold and as direct as Millicent or Seren. Gaia could even face the truth. "I forgive you for not feeling the same."

She'd said it, and didn't crumble when he didn't respond in kind. Maybe this was best. With the release of a pent-up breath, she added, "I wish you well."

He chuckled, the notes sounding odd for Elliot's laugh. "Has a prayer wrought this transformation? Well, He works in mysterious ways."

Maybe it was all the prayers over the years that built up her strength. Amazing. Elliot didn't love her, and no tears came to her. Well, numbness had its benefit. "Good evening. You can go; my friend Seren will be back soon."

When he finally moved, it was to come closer, near enough she trail her pinkie along the edgings of his domino, but that, too, was a cliff she wasn't ready to jump.

"Gaia, what if I'm not ready to leave?"

Her ears warmed, throbbing with the possibilities of his meaning.

"If I am trapped," his voice dropped to a whisper, "it is by your hands."

Her heart clenched at his words. Elliot never seemed more powerful or more dangerous. "I'd hope I, ah, maybe I should be leaving."

He took a half-step, as if to block her path. His outline remained a blur; a tall, powerful blur. "You've had your say, sweet Gaia. Now it is my turn."

This near, she could smell the sweet starch of his thick cravat and a bit of spice. Her heart beat so loudly. Could he hear it?

He drew a thumb down her cheek. "Pretty lady, your

eyes are red. Your cheeks are swollen. What made you cry so hard? And why didn't you find me?"

Something was different about the tone of his hushed voice. There was pain in it. Did he hurt because Gaia had? Could she have discounted the possibility of Elliot returning affections too quickly?

Something dark and formidable drew her to him like never before. "How could I find you? I didn't know you cared, not until this moment."

His arms went about her, and he cradled her against his side. His fingers lighted in her bun. "I'm fascinated with the curl and color of your hair."

Too many thoughts pressed as a familiar tarragon scent tightened its grip about her heart. "Not course or common—"

His lips met her forehead. His hot breath made her shiver and lean more into him. "Never; that's what I've been trying to tell you."

Heady, and a little intoxicated by the feel of his palms on her waist, she released her mask. It fluttered to the floor. Its pole drummed then went silent on the wood floor. She dropped her lids and raised her chin. "I guess this is when you kiss me. Know the lips of someone who esteems you, not your means or connections."

"A lass as beautiful as you needn't ask or wait for a buffoon to find you alone in a library." His arm tightened about her, and he pulled her beneath his cape. The heat of him made her swoon, dipping her head against his broad chest. He tugged a strand of her curls, forcing her chignon to unravel and trail her back. "Now you look the part of a fairy, an all-knowing auburn-haired Gypsy."

He lifted her chin and pressed his mouth against her sealed lips. However, with less than a few seconds of rapture, he relented and released her shoulders.

She wrapped her arms about his neck and wouldn't release him. "I'm horrible. This is my first kiss. I'm sorry." She buried her face against his waistcoat.

His quickened breath warmed her cheek. "Then it should be memorable." His head dipped forward, with the point of his mask, the delicate paper nose, trailing her brows, nudging her face to his. Slowly drawing a finger across her lips, his smooth nail, the feel of his rough warm skin, made them vibrate, relax, then part. "Trust me, Gaia."

She wanted to nod her consent, but didn't dare move from his sensuous touch.

"Let a real kiss come from a man who covets your friendship, who thinks you are beautiful." He dropped his domino to the floor.

Read more of Unmasked Heart at VanessaRiley.com.

Sneak Peak: The Bargain III

VANESSA RILEY

EPISODE III

THE
BARGAIN

A Port Elizabeth Regency Tale

Episode III of The Bargain
Length: 11 Chapters (30,000 words)
Summary: Secrets Revealed

Excerpt: The Aftermath of a Kiss and the Xhosa

"Captain," Ralston cleared his throat. "She fixed me up and a number of others."

The baron's lips pursed as he nodded. "Miss Jewell is full of surprises."

His hair was wild and loose. He smelled of beach sand and perspiration. Still frowning, he raised Ralston's arm a few inches from the boat's deck. "Looks like you will live."

"Don't know how much good that'll do me here, Captain. We left here with peace. Why? What happened? And Mr. Narvel?"

"I don't know, but I'm going to find the answers." Using Mr. Ralston's good arm, the captain pulled him to stand. "Get yourself below and sleep. I've got men on watch. Our guns are ready this time for any other surprises."

The sailor shrugged as he tested his shoulder, pushing at the wrapped muscles. "Yes, Sir."

Lord Welling leaned down and took Precious's hand. "You've helped enough, Miss Jewell. I want you to go down below."

She shook her head. "There's more I can do up here."

The baron snatched her up by the elbow. "I insist."

Precious shook free and grabbed up the doctoring supplies. "We're probably going to need these again."

Ralston closed his eyes and grunted almost in unison

with Lord Welling before trudging past the other men laying out on the deck, the one's whose injured legs prevented them from going below. With no rain, they'd be alright under the night sky.

Precious looked up into the night sky that looked like black velvet with twinkling diamonds. Such innocence shrouds this place. So opposite the truth.

"Come along, Miss Jewel. Now." The baron's voice sounded of distant thunder, quiet and potent. His patience, his anger, at so many lost this night must be stirring. He again put his hands around her shoulders and swept her forward.

She didn't like to be turned so abruptly, but stopping in her tracks didn't seem right either. So she slowed her steps, dragging her slippers against the planks of the Margeaux. "What are you doing?"

He stopped and swung her around so that she faced him. "I need your help telling Mrs. Narvel. It's not going to be easy telling a pregnant woman that—"

"Her husband has died at the Xhosa's hands." Precious's heart drummed loudly, like a death gait. Staying busy helping the injured delayed the building grief she had for her friend. Oh, how was Clara to take it?

Lord Welling's lips thinned and pressed into a line. "It's never easy telling a woman a difficult truth or waiting for her to admit it."

She caught his gaze. It felt as if the fire within it scorched her. Suddenly, the smell of him, the closeness of his stance made her pulse race. He wasn't talking about Clara, but Precious wasn't ready to admit anything.

And what would he think if she told him that at that

moment with Xhosa bearing down upon them that nothing seemed more right than to dive headlong to save him. No, Lord Welling didn't need that bug in his ear.

But soon, he'd press. He wasn't the kind of man who waited for anything.

He gripped her hand and led her into the darkness where those stars twinkled in his eyes. "Precious, I need to ask you something."

Chin lifting, she pushed past him and headed for the hole and the ladder below. "We need to get to Mrs. Narvel."

She took her time climbing down, making sure of her footing on each rung, then she waited at the bottom for her employer, the man who in the middle of chaos kissed her more soundly than any one ever had.

His boots made a gentle thud as he jumped the last rungs. When he pivoted, he crowded her in the dark corner, towering over her. "You're reckless, Precious."

She backed up until she pressed against the compartment's planked wall. "I'm not the only one. Taking Jonas to a land of killing, that's reckless."

He clutched the wall above each of her shoulders, but he might as well had gripped them with his big hands. There was no escape from the truth he was waiting on.

Leaning within an inch of her, his voice reached a loud scolding tone. "You're reckless. Wanton for danger."

Her face grew warm and she bit down on her traitorous lips, ones that wanted a taste of him again.

His breathing seemed noisier. His hands moved to within inches of her arms, but they didn't sneak about her. No, those fingers stayed flat against the wood, tempting, teasing of comfort. "You could've been killed. Will you ever listen?"

The harshness of his tone riled up her spirit. "Won't do me no good to listen if you're dead. The least you can say is thank you."

He straightened and towed one hand to his neck. Out of habit, she squinted as if he'd strike her, but she knew in her bones that wasn't to happen. The fear of him hurting her was long gone. Only the fright of him acting again on that kiss between them remained. "What am I to do with you?"

Get the next Episode. Look for all the episodes. Join my newsletter to stay informed.

Join My Newsletter, Free Goodies

Thank you for taking the time to read Unveiling Love. If you enjoyed it, please consider telling your friends or posting a short review (Amazon or Goodreads). Word of mouth is an author's best friend and much appreciated. Thank you.

Also, sign up for my newsletter and get the latest news on this series or even a free book. I appreciate your support.

VR

Let me point you to some free books, just for reading this far:

Free Book: The Bargain - Episode I:

Coming to London has given Precious Jewell a taste of freedom, and she will do anything, bear anything, to keep it. Defying her master is at the top of her mind, and she won't let his unnerving charm sway her. Yet, will her restored courage lead her to forsake a debt owed to the grave and a child who is as dear to her as her own flesh?

Gareth Conroy, the third Baron Welling, can neither abandon his upcoming duty to lead the fledgling colony of Port Elizabeth, South Africa nor find the strength to be a good father to his heir. Every look at the boy reminds him of the loss of his wife. Guilt over her death plagues his sleep, particularly when he returns to London. Perhaps the spirit and fine eyes of her lady's maid, Precious Jewell, might offer the beleaguered baron a new reason to dream.

Free Book: A Taste of Traditional Regency Romances: Extended excerpts of Regency novels (Bluestocking League Book 1)

From some of the most beloved authors of Regency romance come stories to delight. These excerpts, set in the time of Jane Austen, will give you a sip of sweet romance and will leave you eager for more.

Gail Eastwood, The Captain's Dilemma: Escaped French war prisoner Alexandre Valmont has risked life and honor in a desperate bid to return home and clear his name. Merissa Pritchard risks charges of treason and her family's safety to help the wounded fugitive. But will they risk their hearts in a most dangerous game of love?

From Camille Elliot, The Spinster's Christmas:

Spinster Miranda Belmoore and naval Captain Gerard Foremont, old childhood friends, meet again for a large Christmas party at Wintrell Hall. Miranda is making plans to escape a life of drudgery as a poor relation in her cousin's household, while Gerard battles bitterness that his career was cut short by the injury to his knee. However, an enemy has infiltrated the family party, bent on revenge and determined that Twelfth Night will end in someone's death ...

April Kihlstrom, The Wicked Groom: When the Duke of Berenford is engaged to marry a woman he's never met, what's a poor man to do? How was he to know she wouldn't appreciate his brilliant scheme?

From Vanessa Riley, Unmasked Heart: Shy, nearsighted caregiver, Gaia Telfair never guessed she couldn't claim her father's love because of a family secret, her illicit birth. Can the mulatto passing for white survive being exposed and shunned by the powerful duke who has taken an interest in her? William St. Landon, the Duke of Cheshire, will do anything to protect his mute daughter from his late wife's scandals. He gains the help of Miss Telfair, who has the ability to help children learn to speak, but with a blackmailer at large, if only he could do a better job at shielding his heart.

Regina Scott, Secrets and Sensibilities: When art teacher Hannah Alexander accompanies her students on a country house visit, she never dreams of entering into a dalliance with the handsome new owner David Tenant. But one moment in his company and she's in danger of losing her heart, and soon her very life.

Join the Bluestocking League in celebrating the wonder of traditional <u>Regency romance</u>.

CPSIA information can be obtained
at www.ICGtesting.com
Printed in the USA
LVHW010041250222
711932LV00003B/421

9 781943 885121